The Task

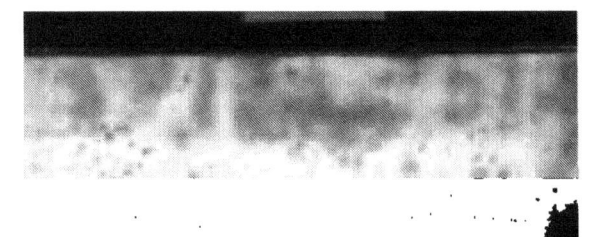

The Cottager's & c.
Mrs. Brown and her Luon's in a distant from
Her Sons, & c.

THE TASK,

A POEM.

IN SIX BOOKS.

BY WILLIAM COWPER,

OF THE INNER TEMPLE, ESQ.

TO WHICH IS PREFIXED,

A Short Account of the

LIFE AND WRITINGS OF THE AUTHOR.

Albany:

PUBLISHED BY B. D. PACKARD, 41 STATE-STREET.

Robert Packard, Printer.

1810.

THE LIFE AND WRITINGS

OF

WILLIAM COWPER, ESQ.

Iт has frequently been observed, that the life of a
man of genius is marked by few incidents. The
mind which grows up amidst the privacies of study,
and the character, which is framed by solitary meditation, belong in a great degree, to a world of their
own, from which the passions and events of ordinary life are equally excluded.   There is, therefore,
nothing very remarkable in the life of the poet to
whom these pages are devoted.   But in the history
of those who have done honor to their country, and
added richness to their native language, no circumstance is trifling, and no incident unworthy of record ;
especially as there is a sort of sanctity attached to
these men, which diffuses itself to the minutest
transaction in which they have been concerned.

Mr. Cowper was born at Berkhamsted, in Buck-
inghamshire, of amiable, and respectable parents, of
noble affinity, and connected with persons of great
worldly influence, his advancement in temporal afflu-
ence and honor, seemed to demand no uncommon

mental endowments.   His opening genius discover-
ed, however, a capacity for elegant literature ; and
he enjoyed the best advantages for improvement, in
so pleasing a pursuit.   With uncommon abilities, he
possessed a most amiable temper ; and he became,
not only the darling of his relations, but beloved and
admired by his associates in education.   But the
towering hopes that were naturally built on so flatter-
ing a ground, were undermined at an early period.
From childhood, during which he lost a much loved
parent, his spirits were always very tender, and often
greatly dejected.   His natural diffidence, and depres-
sion of mind, were increased to a most distressing
degree, by the turbulence of his elder comrades, at
the most celebrated public school in England.   And,
when at mature age, he was appointed to a lucrative
and honorable station in the Law, he shrunk with the
greatest terror, from the appearance which it requir-
ed him to make before the upper house of Parlia-
ment.   Several affecting circumstances concurred
to increase the agony of his mind, while revolving
the consequences of relinquishing the post to which
he had been nominated ; and he wished for a mental
derangement, as the only apparent means by which
his perplexity and distress could be terminated.   A
situation of mind, of which few among mankind can
form a suitable conception, but which it may be hop-
ed, many will regard with tender pity, drove him to
desperation ; and the manner of his preservation in
life, or rather his restoration to it, indicated an unu-
sual interposition of the Providence of God.   His
friends no longer persisted in urging him to retain

his office. It was resigned; and with it his flatter-
ing prospects vanished, and his connections with the
world dissolved.

At this awful crisis, appears to have commenced
Mr. Cowper's serious attention to the ways of God.
Having been educated in the knowledge of the holy
scriptures, and estranged from the fool-hardy arro-
gance which urges unhappy youths to infidelity, he
had constantly retained a reverence for true piety.
His manners were in general decent and amiable;
and the course of pleasures in which he had indulged
himself, being customary with persons in similar
circumstances, he remained insensible of his real
state, till he was brought to reflect upon the guilt of
that action, by which he had nearly plunged himself
into eternity. He now sunk under the horrors of
perdition; and that distraction which he had sought
as a refuge from the fear of man, now seized him
amidst his terrors of eternal judgment....A vein of
self-loathing ran through the whole of his insanity;
and his faculties were so completely deranged, that
the attempt, which he had lately deplored as an un-
pardonable transgression, now appeared to him an
indispensible work of piety. He therefore repeated
his assaults upon his own life, under the dreadful de-
lusion, that it was right to rid the earth of such a
sinner. His purpose being again mercifully frus-
trated, he became at length familiar with despair,
and suffered it to be alleviated by conversation.
And after having endured the severest distress, he
very beautifully describes the consolation which he

A 2

derived from his faith in the Son of God, in the following affecting allegory.

> " I was a stricken deer, that left the herd
> Long since; with many an arrow deep infixt,
> My panting side was charg'd, when I withdrew
> To seek a tranquil death in distant shades.
> There was I found by one who had himself
> Been hurt by th' archers. In his side he bore,
> And in his hands and feet, the cruel scars.
> With gentle force soliciting the darts,
> He drew them forth, and heal'd, and bade me live."

During the last year or two of Mr. Cowper's life, his health, and his state of mind, appeared to be as much restored as for any time during his long afflictions....He was, however, attacked by a disorder, which brought on a rapid decay. Early on the 25th of April, 1800, he sunk into a state of apparent insensibility, which might have been taken for a tranquil slumber, but that his eyes remained half open. His breath was regular, though feeble; and his countenance perfectly serene. In this state he continued for twelve hours: and then expired, without heaving his breath.

The first volume of poems, which he published, consists of various pieces, on various subjects. It seems that he had been assiduous in cultivating a turn for grave and argumentative versification, on moral and ethical topics. Of this kind is the Table Talk, and several other pieces in the collection.

It would be absurd to give one general character of the pieces that were published in this volume : yet this is true concerning Mr. Cowper's productions; that in all the varieties of his style there may still be discerned the likeness and impression of the same mind; the same unaffected modesty which always rejects unseasonable ambitions and ornaments of language; the same easy vigor; the same serene and cheerful hope derived from a steady and unshaken faith in the principles of christianity.

I am not prepared to affirm that Mr. Cowper derives any praise from the choice and elegance of his words; but he has the higher praise of having chosen them without affectation. He appears to have used them as he found them; neither introducing fastidious refinements, nor adhering to obsolete barbarisms. He understands the whole science of numbers, and he has practised their different kinds with considerable happiness; and if his verses do not flow so softly as the delicacy of a modern ear requires, that roughness, which is objected to his poetry, is his choice, not his defect. But this sort of critics, who admire only what is exquisitely polished, these lovers of " gentleness without sinews,"* ought to take into their estimate the vast effusion of thought which is so abundantly poured over the writings of Mr. Cowper, without which human discourse is only an idle combination of sounds and syllables.

After an interval of a few years, his TASK was ushered into the world. The occasion that gave birth to it was a trivial one. A lady had requested

* Dr. Sprat's Life of Cowley.

him to write a piece of blank verse, and gave him
the SOFA for a subject. This he expanded into one
of the finest moral poems of which the English language has been productive.

It is written in blank verse, of which the construction, though in some respects resembling Milton's,
is truly original and characteristic. It is not too
stately for familiar description, nor too depressed for
sublime and elevated imagery. If it has any fault,
it is that of being too much laden with idiomatic ex-
pressions, a fault which the author, in the rapidity
with which his ideas and his utterance seem to have
flowed, very naturally incurred.

In this poem his fancy ran with the most excursive freedom. The poet enlarges upon his topics,
and confirms his argument by every variety of illus-
tration. He never, however, dwells upon them too
long, and leaves off in such a manner, that it seems,
it was in his power to have said more.

The arguments of the poem are various. The
works of nature, the associations with which they
exhibit themselves, the designs of Providence and
the passions of men. Of one advantage the writer
has amply availed himself. The work not being
rigidly confined to any precise subject, he has indulged himself in all the laxity and freedom of a miscel-
laneous poem. Yet he has still adhered so faithful-
ly to the general laws of congruity, that whether he
inspires the softer affections into his reader, or de-

lights him with keen and playful raillery, or discourses on the ordinary manners of human nature, or holds up the bright pictures of religious consolation to his mind, he adopts, at pleasure, a diction just and appropriate, equal in elevation to the sacred effusions of Christian rapture, and sufficiently easy and familiar for descriptions of domestic life; skilful alike in soaring without effort and descending without meanness.

He who desires to put into the hands of youth a poem, which, not destitute of poetic embellishment, is free from all matter of licentious tendency, will find in the Task a book adapted to his purpose. It would be the part of an absurd and extravagant austerity, to condemn those poetical productions in which the passion of love constitutes the primary feature.... In every age that passion has been the concernment of life, the theme of the poet, the plot of the stage. Yet there is a sort of amorous sensibility, bordering almost on morbid enthusiasm, which the youthful mind too frequently imbibes from the glowing sentiments of the poets. Their genius describes, in the most splendid colours, the operations of a passion which requires rebuke instead of incentive, and leads to the most grovelling sensuality the enchantments of a rich and creative imagination. But in the Task of Cowper, there is no licentiousness of description. All is grave, and majestic, and moral. A vein of religious thinking pervades every page, and he discourses, in a strain of the most finished poetry, on the insufficiency and vanity of human pursuits.

Nor is he always severe.   He is perpetually en-
livening the mind of his readers by sportive descriptions, and by representing, in elevated measure, ludicrous objects and circumstances, a species of the
mock-heroic of which Philips was the first author.
In this latter sort of style Mr. Cowper has displayed
great powers of versification, and great talents for
humor.   Of this the historical account he has given
of chairs, in the first book of the Task, is a striking
specimen.

The attention, however, is the most detained by
those passages, in which the charms of rural life, and
the endearments of domestic retirement, are pour-
trayed.   It is in vain to search in any poet of ancient
or modern times for more pathetic touches of representation.   The Task abounds with incidents, intro--
duced as episodes, and interposing an agreeable relief
to the grave and serious parts of the poetry.   Who
has not admired his crazy Kate?   A description in
which the calamity of a disordered reason is painted
with admirable exactness and simplicity.

" She begs an idle pin of all she meets."

I know of no poets who would have introduced so
minute a circumstance into his representation; yet
who is there that does not perceive that it derives its
effect altogether from the minuteness with which it
is drawn?

It were an endless task to point out the beauties
of the poem.   It is now established in its reputation,
and, by universal consent, it has given Cowper a
very high place among the English poets.

THE TASK,

A POEM.

BOOK I.

.

ARGUMENT OF THE FIRST BOOK.

Historical deduction of seats, from the stool to the Sofa....A school
boy's ramble....A walk in the country....The scene described....
Rural sounds as well as sights delightful....Another walk....Mis-
take concerning the charms of solitude corrected....Colonnades
commended....Alcove, and the view from it....The wilderness....
The grove....The thresher....The necessity and the benefits of
exercise....The works of nature superior to, and in some in-
stances inimitable by, art....The wearisomeness of what is com-
monly called a life of pleasure....Change of scene sometimes ex-
pedient....A common described, and the character of Crazy Kate
introduced....Gipsies....The blessings of civilized life....That state
most favorable to virtue....The South Sea islanders compassion-
ated, but chiefly Omai....His present state of mind supposed....
Civilized life friendly to virtue, but not great cities....Great cities,
and London in particular, allowed their due praise, but censured....Fete champetre....The book concludes with a reflection on
the fatal effects of dissipation and effeminacy upon our public
measures.

THE TASK.

BOOK I.

THE SOFA.

I sing the sofa. I, who lately sang
Truth, Hope, and Charity,* and touch'd with awe
The solemn chords, and with a trembling hand,
Escap'd with pain from that advent'rous flight,
Now seek repose upon an humbler theme;
The theme though humble, yet august and proud
Th' occasion—for the Fair commands the song.

Time was, when clothing sumptuous or for use,
Save their own painted skins, our sires had none.
As yet black breeches were not; satin smooth,
Or velvet soft, or plush with shaggy pile:
The hardy chief upon the rugged rock
Wash'd by the sea, or on the grav'ly bank
Thrown up by wintry torrents roaring loud,
Fearless of wrong, repos'd his weary strength.
Those barb'rous ages past, succeeded next
The birth-day of invention; weak at first,
Dull in design, and clumsy to perform.
Joint-stools were then created; on three legs

* See Poems, vol. I.

B

Upborne they stood.   Three legs upholding firm
A massy slab, in fashion square or round.
On such a stool immortal Alfred sat,
And sway'd the sceptre of his infant realms :
And such in ancient halls and mansions drear
May still be seen ; but perforated sore,
And drill'd in holes, the solid oak is found,
By worms voracious eating through and through.

At length a generation more refin'd
Improv'd the simple plan ; made three legs four,
Gave them a twisted form vermicular,
And o'er the seat, with plenteous wadding stuff'd,
Induc'd a splendid cover, green and blue,
Yellow and red, of tap'stry richly wrought
And woven close, or needle-work sublime.
There might ye see the piony spread wide,
The full-blown rose, the shepherd and his lass,
Lap-dog and lambkin with black staring eyes,
And parrots with twin cherries in their beak.

Now came the cane from India, smooth and bright
With nature's varnish ; sever'd into stripes
That interlac'd each other, these supplied
Of texture firm a lattice-work, that brac'd
The new machine, and it became a chair.
But restless was the chair ; the back erect
Distress'd the weary loins, that felt no ease ;
The slipp'ry seat betray'd the sliding part
That press'd it, and the feet hung dangling down,
Anxious in vain to find the distant floor.
These for the rich : the rest, whom fate had plac'd

In modest mediocrity, content
With base materials, sat on well-tann'd hides,
Obdurate and unyielding, glassy smooth,
With here and there a tuft of crimson yarn,
Or scarlet crewel, in the cushion fix'd ;
If cushion might be called, what harder seem'd
Than the firm oak of which the frame was form'd.
No want of timber then was felt or fear'd
In Albion's happy isle.   The umber stood
Pond'rous and fix'd by its own massy weight.
But elbows still were wanting; these, some say,
An alderman of Cripplegate contriv'd :
And some ascribe th' invention to a priest,
Burly and big, and studious of his ease.
But, rude at first, and not with easy slope
Receding wide; they press'd against the ribs,
And bruis'd the side ; and, elevated high,
Taught the rais'd shoulders to invade the ears.
Long time elaps'd or e'er our rugged sires
Complain'd, though incommodiously pent in,
And ill at ease behind.   The ladies first
'Gan murmur, as became the softer sex.
Ingenious fancy, never better pleas'd,
Than when employ'd t' accommodate the fair,
Heard the sweet moan with pity, and devis'd
The soft settee; one elbow at each end,
And in the midst an elbow, it receiv'd,
United yet divided, twain at once.
So sit two kings of Brentford on one throne ;
And so two citizens who take the air,
Close pack'd, and smiling, in a chaise and one.
But relaxation of the languid frame,

By soft recumbency of outstretch'd limbs,
Was bliss reserv'd for happier days. So slow
The growth of what is excellent; so hard
T' attain perfection in this nether world.
Thus first necessity invented stools,
Convenience next suggested elbow chairs,
And luxury th' accomplished SOFA last.

  The nurse sleeps sweetly, hir'd to watch the sick,
Whom snoring she disturbs. As sweetly he
Who quits the coach-box at the midnight hour
To sleep within the carriage more secure,
His legs depending at the open door.
Sweet sleep enjoys the curate in his desk,
The tedious rector drawling o'er his head;
And sweet the clerk below. But neither sleep
Of lazy nurse, who snores the sick man dead,
Nor his who quits the box at midnight hour
To slumber in the carriage more secure,
Nor sleep enjoy'd by curate in his desk,
Nor yet the dosings of the clerk, are sweet,
Compar'd with the repose the SOFA yields.
Oh may I live exempted (while I live
Guiltless of pamper'd appetite obscene)
From pangs arthritic, that infest the toe
Of libertine excess. The SOFA suits
The gouty limb, 'tis true; but gouty limb,
Though on a SOFA, may I never feel:
For I have lov'd the rural walk through lanes
Of grassy swarth, close cropt by nibbling sheep,
And skirted thick with intertexture firm
Of thorny boughs; have lov'd the rural walk

O'er hills, through valleys, and by rivers' brink,
Ere since a truant boy I pass'd my bounds
T' enjoy a ramble on the banks of Thames;
And still remember, nor without regret
Of hours that sorrow since has much endear'd,
How oft, my slice of pocket store consum'd,
Still hung'ring, pennyless and far from home,
I fed on scarlet hips and stony haws,
Or blushing crabs, or berries, that imboss
The bramble, black as jet, or slocs austere.
Hard fare! but such as boyish appetite
Disdains not; nor the palate, undeprav'd
By culinary arts, unsav'ry deems.
No sofa then awaited my return;
Nor sofa then I needed.   Youth repairs
His wasted spirits quickly, by long toil
Incurring short fatigue; and, though our years
As life declines speed rapidly away,
And not a year but pilfers as he goes
Some useful grace that age would gladly keep:
A tooth or auburn lock, and by degrees
Their length and colour from the locks they spare:
Th' elastic spring of an unwearied foot
That mounts the stile with ease, or leaps the fence,
That play of lungs, inhaling and again
Respiring freely the fresh air, that makes
Swift pace or steep ascent no toil to me,
Mine have not pilfer'd yet; nor yet impair'd
My relish of fair prospect; scenes that sooth'd
Or charm'd me young, no longer young, I find
Still soothing, and of pow'r to charm me still.
And witness, dear companion of my walks,
                    B 2

Whose arm this twentieth winter I perceive
Fast lock'd in mine, with pleasure such as love,
Confirm'd by long experience of thy worth
And well-tried virtues, could alone inspire....
Witness a joy that thou hast doubled long.
Thou know'st my praise of nature most sincere,
And that my raptures are not conjur'd up
To serve occasions of poetic pomp,
But genuine, and art partner of them all.
How oft upon yon eminence our pace
Has slacken'd to a pause, and we have borne
The ruffling wind, scarce conscious that it blew,
While admiration, feeding at the eye,
And still unsated, dwelt upon the scene.
Thence with what pleasure have we just descern'd
The distant plough slow moving, and beside
His lab'ring team, that swerv'd not from the track,
The sturdy swain diminish'd to a boy!
Here Ouse, slow winding through a level plain
Of spacious meeds with cattle sprinkled o'er,
Conducts the eye along his sinuous course
Delighted.   There, fast rooted in their bank,
Stand, never overlook'd, our fav'rite elms,
That screen the herdsman's solitary hut;
While far beyond, and overthwart the stream,
That, as with molten glass, inlays the vale,
The sloping land recedes into the clouds ;
Displaying on its varied side the grace
Of hedge-row beauties numberless, square tow'r,
Tall spire, from which the sound of cheerful bells
Just undulates upon the list'ning ear,
Groves, heaths, and smoking villages, remote.

Scenes must be beautiful, which, daily view'd,
Please daily, and whose novelty survives
Long knowledge and the scrutiny of years.
Praise justly due to those that I describe:

   Nor rural sights alone, but rural sounds,
Exhilerate the spirit, and restore
The tone of languid nature.   Mighty winds,
That sweep the skirt of some far-spreading wood
Of ancient growth, make music not unlike
The dash of ocean on his winding shore,
And lull the spirit while they fill the mind;
Unnumber'd branches waving in the blast,
And all their leaves fast flutt'ring, all at once.
Nor less composure waits upon the roar
Of distant floods, or on the softer voice
Of neighb'ring fountain, or of rills that slip
Through the cleft rock, and, chiming as they fall
Upon loose pebbles, lose themselves at length
In matted grass, that with a livelier green
Betrays the secret of their silent course.
Nature inanimate employs sweet sounds,
But animated nature sweeter still,
To sooth and satisfy the human ear.
Ten thousand warblers cheer the day, and one
The livelong night: nor these alone, whose notes
Nice finger'd art must emulate in vain;
But cawing rooks, and kites that swim sublime
In still repeated circles, screaming loud,
The jay, the pie, and ev'n the boding owl,
That hails the rising moon, have charms for me.
Sounds inharmonious in themselves and harsh,

Yet heard in scenes where peace forever reigns,.
And only there, please highly for their sake.

Peace to the artist, whose ingenious thought
Devis'd the weather-house, that useful toy !
Fearless of humid air and gathering rains,
Forth steps the man....an emblem of myself !-
More delicate, his tim'rous mate retires.
When winter soaks the fields, and female feet,.
Too weak to struggle with tenacious clay,
Or ford the rivulets, are best at home,
The task of new discov'ries falls on me.
At such a season, and with such a charge,
Once went I forth ; and found, till then unknown,
A cottage, whither oft we since repair;
'Tis perch'd upon the green-hill top, but close
Environ'd with a ring of branching elms
That overhang the thatch, itself unseen
Peeps at the vale below ; so thick beset
With foilage of such dark redundant growth,
I call'd the low-roof'd lodge the *peasant's nest*.
And, hidden as it is, and far remote
From such unpleasing sounds as haunt the ear
In village or in town, the bay of curs
Incessant, clinking hammers, grinding wheels,
And infants clam'rous whether pleas'd or pain'd,
Oft have I wish'd the peaceful covert mine.
Here, I have said, at least I should possess
The poet's treasure, silence, and indulge
The dreams of fancy, tranquil and secure.
Vain thought ! the dweller in that still retreat
Dearly obtains the refuge it affords.

Its elevated site forbids the wretch
To drink sweet waters of the crystal well;
He dips his bowl into the weedy ditch,
And, heavy laden, brings his bev'rage home,
Far fetch'd and little worth; nor seldom waits,
Dependent on the baker's punctual call,
To hear his creaking panniers at the door,
Angry and sad, and his last crust consum'd.
So farewel envy of the *peasant's nest!*
If solitude make scant the means of life,
Society for me!....thou seeming sweet,
Be still a pleasing object in my view;
My visit still, but never mine abode.

Not distant far, a length of colonnade
Invites us, monument of ancient taste,
Now scorn'd, but worthy of a better fate.
Our fathers knew the value of a screen
From sultry suns; and, in their shaded walks
And long-protracted bow'rs, enjoy'd at noon
The gloom and coolness of declining day.
We bear our shades about us; self-depriv'd
Of other screen, the thin umbrella spread,
And range an Indian waste without a tree.
Thanks to Benevolus*....he spares me yet
These chesnuts rang'd in corresponding lines;
And, though himself so polish'd, still reprieves
The obsolete prolixity of shade.

Descending now (but cautious, lest too fast)
A sudden steep, upon a rustic bridge

* John Courtney Throckmorton, Esq. of Weston Underwood.

We pass a gulf, in which the willows dip
Their pendant boughs, stooping as if to drink.
Hence, ancle-deep in moss and flow'ry thyme,
We mount again, and feel at ev'ry step
Our foot half sunk in hillocks green and soft,
Rais'd by the mole, the miner of the soil.
He, not unlike the great ones of mankind,
Disfigures earth ; and, plotting in the dark,
Toils much to earn a monumental pile,
That may record the mischiefs he has done.

The summit gain'd, behold the proud alcove
That crowns it ! yet not all its pride secures
The grand retreat from injuries impress'd
By rural carvers, who with knives deface
The pannels, leaving an obscure, rude name,
In characters uncouth, and spelt amiss.
So strong the zeal t' immortalize himself
Beats in the breast of man, that ev'n a few,
Few transient years, won from th' abyss abhorr'd
Of black oblivion, seem a glorious prize,
And even to a clown. Now roves the eye :
And posted on this speculative height,
Exults in its command. The sheep-fold here
Pours out its fleecy tenants o'er the glebe.
At first, progressive as a stream, they seek
The middle field ; but scatter'd by degrees,
Each to his choice, soon whiten all the land.
There, from the sun-burnt hay-field, homeward
        creeps
The loaded wain ; while, lighten'd of its charge,
The wain that meets it passes swiftly by ;

The boorish driver leaning o'er his team
Vocif'rous, and impatient of delay.
Nor less attractive is the woodland scene,
Diversified with trees of ev'ry growth,
Alike, yet various.   Here the gray smooth trunks
Of ash, or lime, or beech, distinctly shine,
Within the twilight of their distant shades;
There, lost behind a rising ground, the wood
Seems sunk, and shorten'd to its topmost boughs.
No tree in all the grove but has its charms,
Though each its hue peculiar; paler some,
And of a wannish gray; the willow such,
And poplar, that with silver lines his leaf,
And ash far-stretching his umbrageous arm.
Of deeper green the elm; and deeper still,
Lord of the woods, the long-surviving oak.
Some glossy leav'd, and shining in the sun,
The maple, and the beach of oily nuts
Prolific, and the lime at dewy eve
Diffusing odors: nor unnoted pass
The sycamore, capricious in attire,
Now green, now tawny, and, ere autumn yet
Have chang'd the woods, in scarlet honors bright.
O'er these, but far beyond (a spacious map
Of hill and valley interpos'd between)
The Ouse, dividing the well-water'd land,
Now glitters in the sun, and now retires,
As bashful, yet impatient to be seen.

Hence the declivity is sharp and short,
And such the re-ascent; between them weeps
A little Naiad her impoverish'd urn

All summer long, which winter fills again.
The folded gates would bar my progress now,
But that the Lord* of this enclos'd demesne,
Communicative of the good he owns,
Admits me to a share ; the guiltless eye
Commits no wrong, nor wastes what it enjoys.
Refreshing change ! where now the blazing sun ?
By short transition we have lost his glare,
And stepp'd at once into a cooler clime.
Ye fallen avenues ! once more I mourn
Your fate unmerited, once more rejoice
That yet a remnant of your race survives.
How airy and how light the graceful arch,
Yet awful as the consecrated roof
Re-echoing pious anthems ! while beneath
The chequer'd earth seems restless as a flood
Brush'd by the wind.   So sportive is the light
Shot through the boughs, it dances as they dance,
Shadow and sunshine intermingling quick,
And dark'ning and enlight'ning, as the leaves
Play wanton, ev'ry moment, ev'ry spot.

And now, with nerves new brac'd and spirits
        cheer'd,
We tread the wilderness, whose well-roll'd walks,
With curveture of slow and easy sweep....
Deception innocent....give ample space
To narrow bounds.   The grove receives us next;
Between the upright shafts of whose tall elms
We may discern the thrasher at his task.
Thump after thump resounds the constant flail,

* See the foregoing note.

That seems to swing uncertain, and yet falls
Full on the destin'd ear.   Wide flies the chaff.
The rustling straw sends up a frequent mist
Of atoms, sparkling in the noon-day beam.
Come hither, ye that press your beds of down,
And sleep not: see him sweating o'er his bread
Before he eats it....'Tis the primal curse,
But soften'd into mercy ; made the pledge
Of cheerful days, and nights without a groan.

   By ceaseless action all that is subsists.
Constant rotation of th' unwearied wheel
That nature rides upon, maintains her health,
Her beauty, her fertility.   She dreads
An instant's pause, and lives but while she moves.
Its own revolvency upholds the world.
Winds from all quarters agitate the air,
And fit the limpid element for use,
Else noxious ; oceans, rivers, lakes, and streams,
All feel the fresh'ning impulse, and are cleans'd
By restless undulation : ev'n the oak
Thrives by the rude concussion of the storm :
He seems indeed indignant, and to feel
Th' impression of the blast with proud disdain,
Frowning, as if in his unconscious arm
He held the thunder : but the monarch owes
His firm stability to what he scorns....
More fix'd below, the more disturb'd above.
The law by which all creatures else are bound,
Binds man the lord of all.   Himself derives
No mean advantage from a kindred cause,
From strenuous toil his hours of sweetest ease.

c

} The sedentary stretch their lazy length
When custom bids, but no refreshment find,
For none they need : the languid eye, the cheek
Deserted of its bloom, the flaccid, shrunk,
And wither'd muscle, and yet the vapid soul,
Reproach their owner with that love of rest
To which he forfeits ev'n the rest he loves.
Not such the alert and active.   Measure life
By its true worth, the comforts it affords,
And their's alone seems worthy of the name.
Good health, and, its associate in most,
Good temper ; spirits prompt to undertake,
And not soon spent, though in an arduous task ;
The pow'r of fancy and strong thought are theirs;
Ev'n age itself seems privileg'd in them,
With clear exemption from its own defects.
A sparkling eye beneath a wrinkled front
The vet'ran shows, and, gracing a grey beard
With youthful smiles, descends toward the grave
Sprightly, and old almost without decay.

   Like a coy maiden, ease, when courted most,
Farthest retires....an idol, at whose shrine
Who oft'nest sacrifice are favor'd least.
The love of nature, and the scene she draws,
Is nature's dictate.   Strange! there should be found,
Who, self-imprison'd in their proud saloons,
Renounce the odors of the open field
For the unscented fictions of the loom ;
Who, satisfied with only pencil'd scenes,
Prefer to the performance of a God
Th' inferior wonders of an artist's hand !

Lovely indeed the mimick works of art;
But nature's works far lovelier. I admire....
None more admires....the painter's magic skill,
Who shows me that which I shall never see,
Conveys a distant country into mine,
And throws Italian light on English walls:
But imitative strokes can do no more
Than please the eye....sweet nature ev'ry sense.
The air salubrious of her lofty hills,
The cheering fragrance of her dewy vales,
And music of her woods....no works of man
May rival these; these all bespeak a pow'r
Peculiar, and exclusively her own.
Beneath the open sky she spreads the feast;
'Tis free to all....'tis ev'ry day renew'd;
Who scorns it starves deservedly at home.
He does not scorn it, who, imprison'd long
In some unwholesome dungeon, and a prey
To sallow sickness, which the vapors, dank
And clammy, of his dark abode have bred,
Escapes at last to liberty and light:
His cheek recovers soon its healthful hue;
His eye relumines its extinguish'd fires;
He walks, he leaps, he runs....is wing'd with joy,
And riots in the sweets of ev'ry breeze.
He does not scorn it, who has long endur'd
A fever's agonies, and fed on drugs.
Nor yet the mariner, his blood inflam'd
With acrid salts: his very heart athirst
To gaze at nature in her green array,
Upon the ship's tall side he stands, possess'd
With visions prompted by intense desire:

Fair fields appear below, such as he left
Far distant, such as he would die to find....
He seeks them headlong, and is seen no more.

   The spleen is seldom felt were Flora reigns;
The low'ring eye, the petulence, the frown,
And sullen sadness that o'ershade, distort,
And mar the face of beauty, when no cause
For such immeasurable woe appears,
These Flora banishes, and gives the fair
Sweet smiles, and bloom less transient than her own,
It is the constant revolution, stale
And tasteless, of the same repeated joys,
That palls and satiates, and makes languid life
A pedlar's pack, that bows the bearer down.
Health suffers, and the spirits ebb; the heart
Recoils from its own choice....at the full feast
Is famish'd....finds no music in the song,
No smartness in the jest; and wonders why.
Yet thousands still desire to journey on,
Though halt, and weary of the path they tread.
The paralytic, who can hold her cards,
But cannot play them, borrows a friend's hand
To deal and shuffle, to divide and sort
Her mingled suits and sequences; and sits,
Spectatress both and spectacle, a sad
And silent cypher, while her proxy plays.
Others are dragg'd into the crowded room
Between supporters; and, once seated, sit,
Through downright inability to rise,
Till the stout bearers lift the corpse again.
These speak a loud memento. Yet ev'n these

Themselves love life, and cling to it, as he
That overhangs a torrent, to a twig.
They love it, and yet loath it ; fear to die,
Yet scorn the purposes for which they live.
Then wherefore not renounce them? No....the dread,
The slavish dread of solitude, that breeds
Reflection and remorse, the fear of shame,
And their invet'rate habits, all forbid.

Whom call we gay ? That honor has been long
The boast of mere pretenders to the name.
The innocent are gay....the lark is gay,
That dries his feathers, saturate with dew,
Beneath the rosy cloud, while yet the beams
Of day-spring overshoot his humble nest.
The peasant too, a witness of his song,
Himself a songster, is as gay as he.
But save me from the gaiety of those
Whose head-aches nail them to a noon-day bed ;
And save me too from theirs whose haggard eyes
Flash desperation, and betray their pangs
For property stripp'd off by cruel chance ;
From gaiety that fills the bones with pain,
The mouth with blasphemy, the heart with woe.

The earth was made so various, that the mind
Of desultory man, studious of change,
And pleas'd with novelty, might be indulg'd.
Prospects, however lovely, may be seen
Till half their beauties fade ; the weary sight,
Too well acquainted with their smiles, slides off,
Fastidious, seeking less familiar scenes.
                c 2

Then snug enclosures in the shelter'd vale,
Where frequent hedges intercept the eye,
Delight us; happy to renounce awhile,
Not senseless of its charms, what still we love,
That such short absence may endear it more.
Then forests, or the savage rock, may please,
That hides the sea-mew in his hollow clefts
Above the reach of man. His hoary head,
Conspicuous many a league, the mariner,
Bound homeward, and in hope already there,
Greets with three cheers exulting. At his waist
A girdle of half-wither'd shrubs he shows,
And at his feet the baffled billows die.
The common, overgrown with fern, and rough
With prickly gorse, that, shapeless and deform'd,
And dang'rous to the touch, has yet its bloom,
And decks itself with ornaments of gold,
Yields no unpleasing ramble; there the turf
Smells fresh, and, rich in odorif'rous herbs
And fungous fruits of earth, regales the sense
With luxury of unexpected sweets.

There often wanders one, whom better days
Saw better clad, in cloak of satin, trimm'd
With lace, and hat with splendid ribbon round.
A serving maid was she, and fell in love
With one who left her, went to sea, and died.
Her fancy follow'd him through foaming waves
To distant shores; and she would sit and weep
At what a sailor suffers; fancy, too,
Delusive most were warmest wishes are,
Would oft anticipate his glad return,

And dream of transports she was not to know.
She heard the doleful tidings of his death....
And never smil'd again ! and now she roams
The dreary waste ; there spends the livelong day,
And there, unless when charity forbids,
The livelong night.   A tatter'd apron hides,
Worn as a cloak, and hardly hides, a gown
More tatter'd still ; and both but ill conceal
A bosom heav'd with never-ceasing sighs.
She begs an idle pin of all she meets,
And hoards them in her sleeve ; but needful food
Though press'd with hunger oft, or comelier clothes,
Though pinch'd with cold, asks never.....Kate is
    craz'd !

   I see a column of slow rising smoke
O'ertop the lofty wood that skirts the wild.
A vagabond and useless tribe there eat
Their miserable meal.   A kettle, slung
Between two poles upon a stick transverse,
Receives the morsel....flesh obscene of dog,
Or vermin, or, at best, of cock purloin'd
From his accustom'd perch.   Hard-faring race !
They pick their fuel out of ev'ry hedge,
Which, kindled with dry leaves, just saves un-
    quench'd
The spark of life.   The sportive wind blows wide
Their flutt'ring rags, and shows a tawny skin,
The vellum of the pedigree they claim.
Great skill have they in palmistry, and more
To conjure clean away the gold they touch,
Conveying worthless dross into its place ;

Loud when they beg, dumb only when they steal. '
Strange! that a creature rational, and cast
In human mould, should brutalize by choice
His nature ; and, though capable of arts
By which the world might profit, and himself,
Self-banish'd from society, prefer
Such squalid sloth to honorable toil !
Yet even these, though, feigning sickness oft,
They swathe the forehead, drag the limping limb,
And vex their flesh with artificial sores ;
Can change their whine into a mirthful note
When safe occasion offers ; and, with dance,
And music of the bladder and the bag,
Beguile their woes, and make the woods resound.
Such health and gaiety of heart enjoy
The houseless rovers of the sylvan world ;
And, breathing wholesome air, and wand'ring much,
Need other physic none to heal th' effects
Of loathsome diet, penury, and cold.

   Blest he, though undistinguish'd from the crowd
By wealth or dignity, who dwells secure
Where man, by nature fierce, has laid aside
His fierceness, having learnt, though slow to learn,
The manners and the arts of civil life.
His wants, indeed, are many ; but supply
Is obvious, plac'd within the easy reach
Of temp'rate wishes and industrious hands.
Here virtue thrives as in her proper soil ;
Not rude and surly, and beset with thorns,
And terrible to sight, as when she springs
(If e'er she springs spontaneous) in remote

And barb'rous climes, where violence prevails,
And strength is lord of all; but gentle, kind,
By culture tam'd, by liberty refresh'd,
And all her fruits by radiant truth matur'd.
War and the chase engross the savage whole;
War follow'd for revenge, or to supplant
The envied tenants of some happier spot;
The chase for sustenance, precarious trust!
His hard condition with severe constraint
Binds all his faculties, forbids all growth
Of wisdom, proves a school in which he learns   –
Sly circumvention, unrelenting hate,
Mean self attachment, and scarce aught beside.
Thus fare the shiv'ring natives of the north,
And thus the rangers of the western world,
Where it advances far into the deep,
Towards th' Antarctic.   Ev'n the favor'd isles,
So lately found, although the constant sun
Cheer all their seasons with a grateful smile,
Can boast but little virtue; and, inert
Through plenty, lose in morals what they gain
In manners,....victims of luxurious ease.
These therefore I can pity, plac'd remote
From all that science traces, art invents,
Or inspiration teaches; and enclos'd
In boundless oceans, never to be pass'd
By navigators uninform'd as they,
Or plough'd perhaps by British bark again:
But, far beyond the rest, and with most cause,
Thee, gentle savage!* whom no love of thee
Or thine, but curiosity perhaps,

* Omai.

Or else vain glory, prompted us to draw
Forth from thy native bow'rs, to show thee here
With what superior skill we can abuse
The gifts of Providence, and squander life.
The dream is past ; and thou hast found again
Thy cocoas and bananas, palms and yams,
And home-stall thatch'd with leaves.   But hast thou
        found
Their former charms ? And, having seen our state,
Our palaces, our ladies, and our pomp
Of equipage, our gardens, and our sports,
And heard our music ; are thy simple friends,
Thy simple fare, and all thy plain delights,
As dear to thee as once ? And have thy joys
Lost nothing in comparison with ours ?
Rude as thou art, (for we return the rude
And ignorant, except of outward show)
I cannot think thee yet so dull of heart
And spiritless, as never to regret
Sweets tasted here, and left as soon as known.
Methinks I see thee straying on the beach,
And asking of the surge that bathes thy foot,
If ever it has wash'd our distant shore.
I see thee weep, and thine are honest tears,
A patriot's for his country : thou art sad
At thought of her forlorn and abject state,
From which no power of thine can raise her up.
Thus fancy paints thee, and, though apt to err,
Perhaps errs little when she paints thee thus.
She tells me, too, that duly ev'ry morn
Thou climb'st the mountain top, with eager eye
Exploring far and wide the wat'ry waste

For sight of ship from England. Ev'ry speck
Seen in the dim horizon turns thee pale
With conflict of contending hopes and fears.
But comes at last the dull and dusky eve,
And sends thee to thy cabin, well prepar'd
To dream all night of what the day denied.
Alas! expect it not. We found no bait
To tempt us in thy country. Doing good,
Disinterested good, is not our trade.
We travel far, 'tis true, but not for nought;
And must be brib'd, to compass earth again,
By other hopes and richer fruits than yours.

But, though true worth and virtue in the mild
And genial soil of cultivated life
Thrive most, and may perhaps thrive only there,
Yet not in cities oft: in proud, and gay,
And gain-devoted cities. Thither flow
As to a common and most noisome sewer,
The dregs and feculence of ev'ry land.
In cities foul example on most minds
Begets its likeness. Rank abundance breeds
In gross and pamper'd cities, sloth and lust,
And wantonness and gluttonous excess.
In cities vice is hidden with most ease,
Or seen with least reproach; and virtue, taught
By frequent lapse, can hope no triumph there
Beyond th' achievement of successful flight.
I do confess them nurs'ries of the arts,
In which they flourish most; where, in the beams
Of warm encouragement, and in the eye
Of public note, they reach their perfect size.

Such London is, by taste and wealth proclaim'd
The fairest capital of all the world,
By riot and incontinence the worst.
There, touch'd by Reynolds, a dull blank becomes
A lucid mirror, in which nature sees
All her reflected features.   Bacon there
Gives more than female beauty to a stone,
And Chatham's eloquence to marble lips.
Nor does the chissel occupy alone
The pow'rs of sculpture, but the style as much;
Each province of her art her equal care.
With nice incision of her guided steel
She ploughs a brazen field, and clothes a soil
So sterile with what charms so'er she will,
The richest scenery and the loveliest forms.
Where finds philosophy her eagle eye,
With which she gazes at yon burning disk
Undazzled, and detects and counts his spots?
In London.   Where her implements exact,
With which she calculates, computes, and scans,
All distance, motion, magnitude, and now
Measures an atom, and now girds a world?
In London.   Where has commerce such a mart,
So rich, so throng'd, so drain'd, and so supplied,
As London....opulent, enlarg'd, and still
Increasing, London? Babylon of old
Not more the glory of the earth than she,
A more accomplish'd world's chief glory now.

      She has her praise.   Now mark a spot or two,
That so much beauty would do well to purge;
And show this queen of cities, that so fair

May yet be foul; so witty, yet not wise.
It is not seemly, nor of good report,
That she is slack in discipline; more prompt
T' avenge than to prevent the breach of law;
That she is rigid in denouncing death
On petty robbers, and indulges life
And liberty, and oft times honor too,
To peculators of the public gold:
That thieves at home must hang; but he that puts
Into his overgorg'd and bloated purse
The wealth of Indian provinces, escapes.
Nor is it well, nor can it come to good,
That, though profane and infidel contempt
Of holy writ, she has presum'd t' annul
And abrogate, as roundly as she may,
The total ordinance and will of God;
Advancing fashion to the post of truth,
And cent'ring all authority in modes
And customs of her own, till sabbath rites
Have dwindled into unrespected forms,
And knees and hassocks are well nigh divorc'd.

    God made the country, and man made the town.
What wonder then that health and virtue, gifts
That can alone make sweet the bitter draught
That life holds out to all, should most abound
And least be threaten'd in the fields and groves?
Possess ye, therefore, ye, who, borne about
In chariots and sedans, know no fatigue
But that of idleness, and taste no scenes
But such as art contrives, possess ye still
Your element; there only can ye shine;
                    D

... ...eeping leaves, is all the light tl
lirds warbling all the music. We ca
The splendor of your lamps; they bu
)ur softer satellite. Your songs conf(
)ur more harmonious notes: the thru
car'd, and th' offended nightingale is
There is a public mischief in your mir
: plagues your country. Folly such a
Irac'd with a sword, and worthier of a
las made, what enemies could ne'er h(
)ur arch of empire, stedfast but for yo
t mutilated structure, soon to fall.

Are occupations of the poet's mind
So pleasing, and that steal away the thought
With such address from themes of sad import,
That, lost in his own musings, happy man!
He feels th' anxieties of life, denied
Their wonted entertainment, all retire.
Such joys has he that sings. But ah! not such,
Or seldom such, the hearers of his song.
Fastidious, or else listless, or perhaps
Aware of nothing arduous in a task
They never undertook, they little note
His dangers or escapes, and haply find
Their least amusement where he found the most.
But is amusement all? studious of song,
And yet ambitious not to sing in vain,
I would not trifle merely, though the world
Be loudest in their praise who do no more.
Yet what can satire, whether grave or gay?
It may correct a foible, may chastise
The freaks of fashion, regulate the dress,
Retrench a sword-blade, or displace a patch;
But where are its sublimer trophies found?
What vice has it subdued? whose heart reclaim'd
By rigor, or whom laugh'd into reform?
Alas! Liviathan is not so tam'd:
Laugh'd at, he laughs again; and, stricken hard,
Turns to the stroke his adamantine scales,
That fear no discipline of human hands.

     The pulpit, therefore (and I name it fill'd
With solemn awe, that bids me well beware
With what intent I touch that holy thing)....

ARGUMENT OF THE SECOND BOOK.

Reflections suggested by the conclusion of the former book....Peace among the nations recommended, on the ground of their common fellowship in sorrow.....Prodigies enumerated.....Sicilian earthquakes....Man rendered obnoxious to these calamities by sin....God the agent in them....The philosophy that stops at secondary causes reproved....Our own late miscarriages accounted for....Satirical notice taken of our trips to Fontainbleau.....But the pulpit, not satire, the proper engine of reformation....The Reverend Advertiser of engraved sermons....Petitmaitre Parson.... The good preacher....Pictures of a theatrical clerical coxcomb.... Story-tellers and jesters in the pulpit reproved....Apostrophe to popular applause....Retailers of ancient philosophy expostulated with....Sum of the whole matter....Effects of sacerdotal mismanagement on the laity....Their folly and extravagance....The mischiefs of profusion....Profusion itself, with all its consequent evils, ascribed, as to its principal cause, to the want of discipline in the universities.

THE TASK.

BOOK II.

THE TIME-PIECE.

OH for a lodge in some vast wilderness,
Some boundless contiguity of shade,
Where rumor of oppression and deceit,
Of unsuccessful or successful war,
Might never reach me more.   My ear is pain'd,
My soul is sick, with ev'ry day's report
Of wrong and outrage with which earth is fill'd.
There is no flesh in man's obdurate heart,
It does not feel for man; the nat'ral bond
Of brotherhood is sever'd as the flax
That falls asunder at the touch of fire;
He finds his fellow guilty of a skin
Not colour'd like his own! and, having pow'r
T' enforce the wrong, for such a worthy cause
Dooms and devotes him as his lawful prey.
Lands intersected by a narrow frith
Abhor each other.   Mountains interpos'd
Make enemies of nations, who had else,
Like kindred drops, been mingled into one.
Thus man devotes his brother, and destroys;
And, worse than all, and most to be deplor'd
                    D 2

As human nature's broadest, foulest blot,
Chains him, and tasks him, and exacts his sweat
With stripes, that mercy, with a bleeding heart,
Weeps when she sees inflicted on a beast.
Then what is man? And what man, seeing this,
And having human feeling, does not blush,
And hang his head, to think himself a man?
I would not have a slave to till my ground,
To carry me, to fan me while I sleep,   .
And tremble when I wake, for all the wealth
That sinews bought and sold have ever earn'd.
No: dear as freedom is, and in my heart's
Just estimation priz'd above all price,
I had much rather be myself the slave,
And wear the bonds, than fasten them on him.
We have no slaves at home....Then why abroad?
And they themselves, once ferried o'er the wave
That parts us, are emancipate and loos'd.
Slaves cannot breathe in England; if their lungs
Receive our air, that moment they are free;
They touch our country, and their shackles fall.
That's noble, and bespeaks a nation proud
And jealous of the blessing.   Spread it then,
And let it circulate through ev'ry vein
Of all your empire; that when Britain's pow'r
Is felt, mankind may feel her mercy too.

Sure there is need of social intercourse,
Benevolence, and peace, and mutual aid,
Between the nations, in a world that seems
To toll the death-bell of its own decease,
And by the voice of all its elements   . .

To preach the gen'ral doom.* When were the winds
Let slip with such a warrant to destroy?
When did the waves so haughtily o'erleap
Their ancient barriers, deluging the dry?
Fires from beneath, and meteors† from above,
Portentous, unexampled, unexplain'd,
Have kindled beacons in the skies; and th' old
And crazy earth has had her shaking fits
More frequent, and forgone her usual rest.
Is it a time to wrangle, when the props
And pillars of our planet seem to fail,
And nature with a dim and sickly eye‡
To wait the close of all? But grant her end
More distant, and that prophecy demands
A longer respite, unaccomplish'd yet;
Still they are frowning signals, and bespeak
Displeasure in HIS breast who smites the earth
Or heals it, makes it languish or rejoice.
And 'tis but seemly, that, where all deserve
And stand expos'd by common peccancy
To what no few have felt, there should be peace,
And brethren in calamity should love.

Alas for Sicily! rude fragments now
Lie scatter'd where the shapely column stood.
Her palaces are dust. In all her streets
The voice of singing and the sprightly chord
Are silent. Revelry, and dance, and show
Suffer a syncope and solemn pause;

* Alluding to the calamities at Jamaica.   † August 18, 1783.

‡ Alluding to the fog that cover'd both Europe and Asia during
the whole summer of 1783.

While God performs upon the trembling stage
Of his own works, his dreadful part alone.
How does the earth receive him?....With what signs
Of gratulation and delight, her King?
Pours she not all her choicest fruits abroad,
Her sweetest flow'rs, her aromatic gums,
Disclosing paradise where'er he treads?
She quakes at his approach. Her hollow womb,
Conceiving thunders, through a thousand deeps
And fiery caverns, roars beneath his foot.
The hills move lightly, and the mountains smoke,
For he has touch'd them. From th' extremest point
Of elevation down into th' abyss,
His wrath is busy, and his frown is felt.
The rocks fall headlong, and the valleys rise,
The rivers die into offensive pools,
And, charg'd with putrid verdure, breathe a gross
And mortal nuisance into all the air.
What solid was, by transformation strange,
Grows fluid; and the fix'd and rooted earth,
Tormented into billows, heaves and swells,
Or with vortiginous and hidious whirl
Sucks down his prey insatiable. Immense
The tumult and the overthrow, the pangs
And agonies of human and of brute
Multitudes, fugitive on ev'ry side,
And fugitive in vain. The sylvan scene
Migrates uplifted; and, with all its soil
Alighting in far distant fields, finds out
A new possessor, and survives the change.
Ocean has caught the phrenzy, and, upwrought
To an enormous and o'erbearing height,

Not by a mighty wind, but by that voice
Which winds and waves obey, invades the shore
Resistless.   Never such a sudden flood,
Upridg'd so high, and sent on such a charge,
Possess'd an inland scene.   Where now the throng
That press'd the beach, and, hasty to depart,
Look'd to the sea for safety? They are gone,
Gone with the refluent wave into the deep....
A prince with half his people! Ancient tow'rs,
And roofs embattled high, the gloomy scenes
Where beauty oft and letter'd worth consume
Life in the unproductive shades of death,
Fall prone: the pale inhabitants come forth,
And, happy in their unforeseen release
From all the rigors of restraint, enjoy
The terrors of the day that sets them free.
Who then, that has thee, would not hold thee fast,
Freedom! whom they that loose thee so regret,
That ev'n a judgment, making way for thee,
Seems in their eyes a mercy for thy sake.

    Such evil sin hath wrought; and such a flame
Kindled in heav'n, that it burns down to earth,
And, in the furious inquest that it makes
On God's behalf, lays waste his fairest works.
The very elements, though each be meant
The minister of man, to serve his wants,
Conspire against him.   With his breath he draws
A plague into his blood; and cannot use
Life's necessary means, but he must die.
Storms rise t' o'erwhelm him: or, if stormy winds
Rise not, the waters of the deep shall rise,

And, needing none assistance of the storm,
Shall roll themselves ashore, and reach him there.
The earth shall shake him out of all his holds,
Or make his house his grave; nor so content,   .
Shall counterfeit the motions of the flood,
And drown him in her dry and dusty gulphs.
What then! were they the wicked above all,
And we the righteous, whose fast anchor'd isle
Mov'd not, while theirs was rock'd like a light skiff
The sport of ev'ry wave? No: none are clear,
And none than we more guilty.   But, where all
Stand chargeable with guilt, and to the shafts
Of wrath obnoxious, God may choose his mark:
May punish, if he please, the less, to warn
The more malignant.   If he spar'd not them,
Tremble and be amaz'd at thine escape,   ·
Far guiltier England, lest he spare not thee!

    Happy the man who sees a God employ'd
In all the good and ill that chequer life!
Resolving all events, with their effects
And manifold results, into the will
And arbitration wise of the supreme.
Did not his eye rule all things, and intend
The least of our concerns (since from the least
The greatest oft originate;) could chance   .
Find place in his dominion, or dispose
One lawless particle to thwart his plan;
Then God might be surpris'd, and unforeseen
Contingence might alarm him, and disturb
The smooth and equal course of his affairs.   ·
This truth philosophy, though eagle-ey'd

In nature's tendencies, oft overlooks;
And, having found his instrument, forgets,
Or disregards, or, more presumptuous still,
Denies the pow'r that wields it. God proclaims
His hot displeasure against foolish men,
That live an atheist life : involves the heav'n
In tempests; quits his grasp upon the winds,
And gives them all their fury ; bids a plague
Kindle a fiery boil upon the skin,
And putrify the breath of blooming health.
He calls for famine, and the meagre fiend
Blows mildew from between his shrivel'd lips,
And taints the golden ear. He springs his mines,
And desolates a nation at a blast.
Forth steps the spruce philosopher, and tells
Of homogeneal and discordant springs
And principles ; of causes, how they work
By necessary laws their sure effects ;
Of action and re-action. He has found
The source of the disease that nature feels,
And bids the world take heart and banish fear.
Thou fool ! will thy discov'ry of the cause
Suspend th' effect, or heal it ? Has not God
Still wrought by means since first he made the
        world ?
And did he not of old employ his means
To drown it ? What is his creation less
Than a capacious reservoir of means
Form'd for his use, and ready at his will ?
Go, dress thine eyes with eye-salve ; ask of him, `
Or ask of whomsoever he has taught ;
And learn, though late, the genuine cause of all.

As nations, ignorant of God, contrive
A wooden one, so we, no longer taught
By monitors that mother church supplies,
Now make our own.   Posterity will ask
(If e'er posterity see verse of mine)
Some fifty or an hundred lustrums hence,
What was a monitor in George's days ?
My very gentle reader, yet unborn,
Of whom I must needs augur better things,
Since Heav'n would sure grow weary of a world
Productive only of a race like ours,
A monitor is wood....plank shaven thin.
We wear it at our backs.   There closely brac'd
And neatly fitted, it compresses hard
The prominent and most unsightly bones,
And binds the shoulders flat.   We prove its use
Sov'reign and most effectual to secure
A form, not now gymnastic as of yore,
From rickets and distortion, else, our lot.
But thus admonish'd, we can walk erect....
One proof at least of manhood; while the friend
Sticks close, a mentor worthy of his charge.
Our habits, costlier than Lucellus wore,
And by caprice as multiplied as his,
Just please us while the fashion is at full,
But change with ev'ry moon.   The sycophant,
Who waits to dress us, arbitrates their date;
Surveys his fair reversion with keen eye;
Finds one ill made, another obsolete,
This fits not nicely, that is ill conceiv'd;
And, making prize of all that he condemns,
With our expenditure defrays his own.

Variety's the very spice of life,
That gives it all its flavor.   We have run
Through ev'ry change, that fancy at the loom,
Exhausted, has had genius to supply;
And studious of mutation still, discard
A real elegance, a little us'd,
For monstrous novelty and strange disguise.
We sacrifice to dress, till household joys
And comforts cease.   Dress drains our cellar dry,
And keeps our larder lean; puts out our fires;
And introduces hunger, frost and woe,
Where peace and hospitality might reign.
What man that lives, and that knows how to live,
Would fail t' exhibit at the public shows
A form as splendid as the proudest there,
Though appetite raise outcries at the cost?
A man o' th' town dines late, but soon enough,
With reasonable forecast and dispatch,
T' ensure a side-box station at half price.
You think, perhaps, so delicate his dress,
His daily fare as delicate.   Alas!
He picks clean teeth, and busy as he seems
With an old tavern quill, is hungry yet!
The rout is folly's circle, which she draws
With magic wand.   So potent is the spell,
That none, decoy'd into that fatal ring,
Unless by Heaven's peculiar grace, escape.
There we grow early grey, but never wise;
There form connexions, but acquire no friend;
Solicit pleasure, hopeless of success;
Waste youth in occupations only fit
For second childhood, and devote old age

To sports which only childhood could excuse.
There they are happiest who dissemble best
Their weariness; and they the most polite
Who squander time and treasure with a smile,
Though at their own destruction. She, that asks
Her dear five hundred friends, contemns them all,
And hates their coming. They (what can they less!)
Make just reprisals; and, with cringe and shrug,
And bow obsequious, hide their hate of her.
All catch the frenzy, downward from her Grace,
Whose flambeaux flash against the morning skies,
And gild our chamber ceilings as they pass,
To her, who, frugal only that her thrift
May feed excesses she can ill afford,
Is hackney'd home unlacquey'd; who, in haste
Alighting, turns the key in her own door, ·
And, at the watchman's lantern borrowing light,
Finds a cold bed her only comfort left.
Wives beggar husbands, husbands starve their wives,
On fortunes velvet altar off'ring up
Their last poor pittance....fortune, most severe
Of goddesses yet known, and costlier far
Than all that held their routs in Juno's heav'n....
So fare we in this prison-house, the world.
And 'tis a fearful spectacle to see
So many maniacs dancing in their chains.
They gaze upon the links that hold them fast
With eyes of anguish, execrate their lot,
Then shake them in despair, and dance again!

    Now basket up the family of plagues
That waste our vitals; peculation, sale

Of honor, perjury, corruption, frauds
By forgery, by subterfuge of law,
By tricks and lies as num'rous and as keen
As the necessities their authors feel !
Then cast them, closely bundled, ev'ry brat
At the right door.   Profusion is the sire.
Profusion unrestrain'd, with all that's base
In character, has litter'd all the land,
And bred, within the mem'ry of no few,
A priesthood such as Baal's was of old,
A people such as never was till now.
It is a hungry vice :....it eats up all
That gives society its beauty, strength,
Convenience, and security, and use :
Makes men mere vermin, worthy to be trapp'd
And gibbeted as fast as catchpoll claws
Can seize the slipp'ry prey : unties the knot
Of union, and converts the sacred band
That holds mankind together to a scourge.
Profusion, deluging a state with lusts
Of grossest nature and of worst effects,
Prepares it for its ruin: hardens, blinds,
And warps, the consciences of public men,
Till they can laugh at virtue ; mock the fools
That trust them ; and, in the end, disclose a face
That would have shock'd credulity herself,
Unmask'd, vouchsafing this their sole excuse....
Since all alike are selfish, why not they ?
This does profusion, and th' accursed cause
Of such deep mischief has itself a cause.

In colleges and halls, in ancient days,
When learning, virtue, piety, and truth,
Were precious, and inculcated with care,
There dwelt a sage call'd Discipline. His head,
Not yet by time completely silver'd o'er,
Bespoke him past the bounds of freakish youth,
But strong for service still, and unimpair'd.
His eye was meek and gentle, and a smile
Play'd on his lips; and in his speech was heard
Paternal sweetness, dignity, and love.
The occupation dearest to his heart
Was to encourage goodness. He would stroke
The head of modest and ingenuous worth,
That blush'd at his own praise; and press the youth
Close to his side that pleas'd him. Learning grew
Beneath his care, a thriving vig'rous plant;
The mind was well inform'd, the passions held
Subordinate, and diligence was choice.
If e'er it chanc'd, as sometimes chance it must,
That one among so many overleap'd
The limits of control, his gentle eye
Grew stern, and darted a severe rebuke:
His frown was full of terror, and his voice
Shook the delinquent with such fits of awe
As left him not, till penitence had won
Lost favor back again, and clos'd the breach.
But Discipline, a faithful servant long,
Declin'd at length into the vale of years;
A palsy struck his arm; his sparkling eye
Was quench'd in rheums of age; his voice, unstrung,
Grew tremulous, and mov'd derision more
Than rev'rence in perverse rebellious youth.

So colleges and halls neglected much
Their good old friend ; and Discipline at length,
O'erlook'd and unemploy'd, fell sick and died.
Then study languish'd, emulation slept,
And virtue fled.   The schools became a scene
Of solemn farce, where ignorance in stilts,
His cap well lin'd with logic not his own,
With parrot tongue perform'd the scholar's part,
Proceeding soon a graduated dunce.
Then compromise had place, and scrutiny
Became stone-blind ; precedence went in truck,
And he was competent whose purse was so.
A dissolution of all bonds ensued ;
The curbs, invented for the mulish mouth
Of head-strong youth, were broken ; bars and bolts
Grew rusty by disuse ; and massy gates
Forgot their office, op'ning with a touch ;
Till gowns at length are found mere masquerade,
The tassel'd cap and the spruce band a jest,
A mock'ry of the world ! What need of these
For gamesters, jockeys, brothellers impure,
Spendthrifts, and booted sportsmen, oft'ner seen
With belted waist and pointers at their heels,
Than in the bounds of duty ? What was learn'd,
If aught was learn'd in childhood, is forgot ;
And such expense as pinches parents blue,
And mortifies the lib'ral hand of love,
Is squander'd in pursuit of idle sports
And vicious pleasures ; buys the boy a name,
That sits a stigma on his father's house,
And cleaves through life inseparably close
To him that wears it.   What can after-games

Of riper joys, and commerce with the world,
The lewd vain world, that must receive him soon,
Add to such crudition, thus acquir'd,
Where science and where virtue are profess'd?
They may confirm his habits, rivet fast
His folly, but to spoil him is a task
That bids defiance to th' united pow'rs
Of fashion, dissipation, taverns, stews.
Now, blame we most the nurslings or the nurse?
The children, crook'd, and twisted, and deform'd,
Through want of care; or her, whose winking eye
And slumb'ring oscitancy, mars the brood?
The nurse no doubt.   Regardless of her charge,
She needs herself correction; needs to learn,
That it is dangerous sporting with the world,
With things so sacred as a nation's trust,
The nurture of her youth, her dearest pledge.

   All are not such.   I had a brother once....
Peace to the mem'ry of a man of worth,
A man of letters, and of manners too!
Of manners sweet as virtue always wears,
When gay good-nature dresses her in smiles.
He grac'd a college,* in which order yet
Was sacred; and was honor'd, lov'd, and wept,
By more than one, themselves conspicuous there.
Some minds are temper'd happily, and mix'd
With such ingredients of good sense and taste
Of what is excellent in man, they thirst
With such a zeal to be what they approve,
That no restraints can circumscribe them more

        * Bennet College, Cambridge.

Than they themselves by choice, for wisdom's sake;
Nor can example hurt them: what they see
Of vice in others but enhancing more
The charms of virtue in their just esteem.
If such escape contagion, and emerge
Pure, from so foul a pool, to shine abroad,
And give the world their talents and themselves,
Small thanks to those whose negligence or sloth,
Expos'd their inexperience to the snare,
And left them to an undirected choice.

See, then, the quiver broken and decay'd,
In which are kept our arrows! rusting there
In wild disorder, and unfit for use,
What wonder, if discharg'd into the world,
They shame their shooters with a random flight,
Their points obtuse, and feathers drunk with wine!
Well may the church wage unsuccessful war,
With such artill'ry arm'd.   Vice parries wide
Th' undreaded volley with a sword of straw,
And stands an impudent and fearless mark.

Have we not track'd the felon home, and found
His birth-place and his dam? The country mourns....
Mourns, because ev'ry plague that can infest
Society, and that saps and worms the base
Of th' edifice that policy has rais'd,
Swarms in all quarters; meets the eye, the ear,
And suffocates the breath at ev'ry turn.
Profusion breeds them; and the cause itself
Of that calamitous mischief has been found:
Found too, where most offensive, in the skirts

Of the rob'd pedagogue ! Else, let th' arraign'd
Stand up unconscious, and refute the charge.
So, when the Jewish leader stretch'd his arm,
And wav'd his rod divine, a race obscene,
Spawn'd in the muddy beds of Nile, came forth,
Polluting Egypt : gardens, fields, and plains,
Were cover'd with the pest; the streets were fill'd;
The croaking nuisance lurk'd in ev'ry nook ;
Nor palaces, nor even chambers, 'scap'd;
And the land stank....so num'rous was the fry.

THE TASK,

A POEM.

BOOK III.

ARGUMENT OF THE THIRD BOOK.

Self-recollection and reproof....Address to domestic happine
Some account of myself....The vanity of many of their pur
who are reputed wise....Justification of my censures....Divin
lumination necessary to the most expert philosopher....'
question, What is truth? answered by other questions....Dome
happiness addressed again....Few lovers of the country...
tame hare....Occupations of a retired gentleman in his garde
Pruning...Framing...Greenhouse....Sowing of flower-seeds....'
country preferable to the town even in the winter....Reasons
it is deserted at that season....Ruinous effects of gaming an
expensive improvement....Book concludes with an apostro
to the metropolis.

THE TASK.

BOOK III.

THE GARDEN.

As one, who, long in thickets and in brakes
Entangled, winds now this way, and now that,
His devious course uncertain, seeking home ;
Or, having long in miry ways been foil'd
And sore discomfited, from slough to slough
Plunging, and half despairing of escape ;
If chance at length he find a greensward smooth
And faithful to the foot, his spirits rise,
He chirrups brisk his ear-erecting steed,
And winds his way with pleasure and with ease.
So I, designing other themes, and call'd
T' adorn the Sofa with eulogium due,
To tell its slumbers, and to paint its dreams,
Have rambled wide.   In country, city, seat
Of academic fame (howe'er deserv'd)
Long held, and scarcely disengag'd at last.
But now, with pleasant pace, a cleanlier road
I mean to tread.   I feel myself at large,
Courageous, and refresh'd for future toil,
If toil await me, or if dangers new.

Since pulpits fail, and sounding boards reflect
Most part an empty ineffectual sound,
What chance that I, to fame so little known,
Nor conversant with men or manners much,
Should speak to purpose, or with better hope
Crack the satiric thong? 'Twere wiser far
For me, enamor'd of sequester'd scenes,
And charm'd with rural beauty, to repose,
Where chance may throw me, beneath elm or vine
My languid limbs, when summer sears the plains;
Or, when rough winter rages, on the soft
And shelter'd Sofa, while the nitrous air
Feeds a blue flame, and makes a cheerful hearth;
There, undisturb'd by folly, and appriz'd
How great the danger of disturbing her,
To muse in silence, or at least confine
Remarks that gall so many to the few
My partner's in retreat. Disgust conceal'd
Is oft times proof of wisdom, when the fault
Is obstinate, and cure beyond our reach.

Domestic happiness, thou only bliss
Of paradise that has surviv'd the fall!
Though few now taste thee unimpair'd and pure,
Or, tasting, long enjoy thee; too infirm,
Or too incautious, to preserve thy sweets
Unmix'd with drops of bitter, which neglect,
Or temper sheds into thy chrystal cup.
Thou art the nurse of virtue....In thine arms
She smiles, appearing, as in truth she is,
Heav'n-born, and destin'd to the skies again.
Thou art not known where pleasure is ador'd,

That reeling goddess with a zoneless waist
And wand'ring eyes, still leaning on the arm
Of novelty, her fickle frail support;
For thou art meek ond constant, hating change,
And, finding, in the calm of truth-tried love,
Joys that her stormy raptures never yield.
Forsaking thee, what shipwreck have we made
Of honor, dignity, and fair renown!
Till prostitution elbows us aside
In all our crowded streets; and senates seem
Conven'd for purposes of empire less
Than to release th' adultress from her bond.
The adultress! what a theme for angry verse!
What provocation to th' indignant heart
That feels for injur'd love! but I disdain
The nauseous task to paint her as she is,
Cruel, abandon'd, glorying in her shame!
No:....let her pass, and chariotted along
In guilty splendor, shake the public ways;
The frequency of crimes has wash'd them white!
And verse of mine shall never brand the wretch,
Whom matrons now, of character unsmirch'd,
And chaste themselves, are not asham'd to own.
Virtue and vice had bound'ries in old time,
Not to be pass'd: and she, that had renounc'd
Her sex's honor, was renounc'd herself
By all that priz'd it; not for prud'ry's sake,
But dignity's, resentful of the wrong.
'Twas hard, perhaps, on here and there a waif,
Desirous to return, and not receiv'd:
But was an wholesome rigor in the main,
And taught th' unblemish'd to preserve with care

6

That purity, whose loss was loss of all. . .
Men, too, were nice in honor in those days
And judg'd offenders well.   Then he that sharp'd,
And pocketed a prize, by fraud obtain'd,
Was mark'd and shun'd as odious.   He that sold
His country, or was slack when she requir'd
His ev'ry nerve in action and at stretch,
Paid, with the blood that he had basely spar'd,
The price of his default.   But now....yes, now,·
We are become so candid and so fair,
So lib'ral in construction, and so rich
In Christian charity, (good-natur'd age!)
That they are safe, sinners of either sex,
Transgress what laws they may.   Well dress'd, well
          bred,
Well equipag'd, is ticket good enough
To pass us readily through ev'ry door.
Hypocrisy, detest her as we may,
(And no man's hatred ever wrong'd her yet)
May claim this merit still....That she admits
The worth of what she mimics with such care,
And thus gives virtue indirect applause;
But she has burnt her mask, not needed here,
Where vice has such allowance, that her shifts
And specious semblances have lost their use.

  I was a stricken deer, that left the herd
Long since; with many an arrow deep infix'd,
My panting side was charg'd, when I withdrew
To seek a tranquil death in distant shades.
There was I found by one who had himself
Been hurt by th' archers.   In his side he bore,

And in his hands and feet, the cruel scars.
With gentle force soliciting the darts,
He drew them forth, and heal'd, and bade me live.
Since then, with few associates, in remote
And silent woods I wander, far from those
My former partners of the peopled scene;
With few associates, and not wishing more.
Here much I ruminate, as much I may,
With other views of men and manners now
Than once, and others of a life to come.
I see that all are wand'rers, gone astray
Each in his own delusions; they are lost
In chase of fancied happiness, still woo'd
And never won.   Dream after dream ensues;
And still they dream that they shall still succeed,
And still are disappointed.   Rings the world
With the vain stir.   I sum up half mankind,
And add two thirds of the remaining half,
And find the total of their hopes and fears
Dreams, empty dreams.   The million flit as gay
As if created only like the fly,
That spreads his motley wings in th' eye of noon,
To sport their season, and be seen no more.
The rest are sober dreamers, grave and wise,
And pregnant with discov'ries new and rare.
Some write a narrative of wars, and feats
Of heroes little known; and call the rant
An history: describe the man, of whom
His own coevals took but little note;
And paint his person, character, and views,
As they had known him from his mother's womb.
They disentangle from the puzzled skein,

In which obscurity has wrapp'd them up,
The threads of politic and shrewd design,
That ran through all his purposes, and charge
His mind with meaning that he never had,
Or, having, kept conceal'd.   Some drill and bore
The solid earth, and from the strata there
Extract a register, by which we learn,
That he who made it, and reveal'd its date
To Moses, was mistaken in its age.
Some, more acute, and more industrious still,
Contrive creation; travel nature up
To the sharp peak of her sublimest height,
And tell us whence the stars; why some are fix'd,
And planetary some; what gave them first
Rotation; from what fountain flow'd their light.
Great contest follows, and much learned dust
Involves the combatants; each claiming truth,
And truth disclaiming both.   And thus they spend
The little wick of life's poor shallow lamp,
In playing tricks with nature, giving laws
To distant worlds, and trifling in their own.
Is't not a pity now, that tickling rheums
Should ever tease the lungs and blear the sight
Of oracles like these? Great pity too,
That, having wielded th' elements, and built
A thousand systems, each in his own way,
They should go out in fume, and be forgot?
Ah! what is life thus spent? and what are they
But frantic, who thus spend it? all for smoke....
Eternity for bubbles, proves at last
A senseless bargain.   When I see such games
Play'd by the creatures of a pow'r who swears

That he will judge the earth, and call the fool
To a sharp reck'ning that has liv'd in vain ;
And when I weigh this seeming wisdom well,
And prove it in th' infallible result
So hollow and so false....I feel my heart
Dissolve in pity, and account the learn'd,
If this be learning, most of all deceiv'd.
Great crimes alarm the conscience, but it sleeps
While thoughtful man is plausibly amus'd.
Defend me, therefore, common sense, say I,
From reveries so airy, from the toil
Of dropping buckets into empty wells,
And growing old in drawing nothing up !

'Twere well, says one sage erudite, profound,
Terribly arch'd and aquiline his nose,
And over-built with most impending brows,
'Twere well, could you permit the world to live
As the world pleases.   What's the world to you ?....
Much.   I was born of woman, and drew milk,
As sweet as charity from human breasts.
I think, articulate, I laugh and weep,
And exercise all functions of a man.
How then should I and any man that lives
Be strangers to each other ? Pierce my vain,
Take of the crimson stream meand'ring there,
And catechise it well ; apply the glass,
Search it, and prove now if it be not blood
Congenial with thine own : and, if it be,
What edge of subtlety canst thou suppose
Keen enough, wise and skilful as thou art,
To cut the link of brotherhood, by which
G 2

One common Maker bound me to the kind?
True; I am no proficient, I confess,
In arts like yours.   I cannot call the swift
And perilous lightnings from the angry clouds,
And bid them hide themselves in earth beneath;
I cannot analyse the air, nor catch
The parallax of yonder luminous point,
That seems half quench'd in the immense abyss:
Such pow'rs I boast not....neither can I rest
A silent witness of the headlong rage
Or heedless folly by which thousands die,
Bone of my bone, and kindred souls to mine.

   God never meant that man should scale the heav'ns
By strides of human wisdom.   In his works,
Though wond'rous, he commands us in his word
To seek HIM rather, where his mercy shines.
The mind, indeed, enlighten'd from above,
Views him in all; ascribes to the grand cause
The grand effect; acknowledges with joy
His manner, and with rapture tastes his style.
But never yet did philosophic tube,
That brings the planets home into the eye
Of observation, and discovers, else
Not visible, his family of worlds,
Discover him that rules them; such a veil
Hangs over mortal eyes, blind from the birth,
And dark in things divine.   Full often, too,
Our wayward intellect, the more we learn
Of nature, overlooks her Author more;
From instrumental causes proud to draw
Conclusions retrograde, and mad mistake.

But if his word once teach us, shoot a ray
Through all the heart's dark chambers, and reveal
Truths undiscern'd but by that holy light,
Then all is plain. Philosophy, baptiz'd.
In the pure fountain of eternal love,
Has eyes, indeed; and viewing all she sees
As meant to indicate a God to man,
Gives him his praise, and forfeits not her own.
Learning has borne such fruit in other days
On all her branches: piety has found
Friends in the friends of science, and true pray'r
Has flow'd from lips wet with Castalian dews.
Such was thy wisdom, Newton, childlike sage!
Sagacious reader of the works of God,
And in his works sagacious. Such too thine,
Milton, whose genius had angelic wings,
And fed on manna! And such thine, in whom
Our British Themis gloried with just cause,
Immortal Hale! for deep discernment prais'd,
And sound integrity, not more than fam'd
For sanctity of manners undefil'd.

All flesh is grass, and all its glory fades
Like the fair flow'r dishevell'd in the wind;
Riches have wings, and grandeur is a dream:
The man we celebrate must find a tomb,
And we that worship him, ignoble graves.
Nothing is proof against the gen'ral curse
Of vanity, that seizes all below.
The only amaranthine flow'r on earth
Is virtue; th' only lasting treasure, truth.
But what is truth? 'twas Pilate's question, put

To truth itself, that deign'd him no reply.
And wherefore? will not God impart his light
To them that ask it?....Freely....'tis his joy,
His glory, and his nature, to impart.
But to the proud, uncandid, insincere,
Or negligent enquirer, not a spark.
What's that which brings contempt upon a book,
And him who writes it; though the style be neat,
The method clear, and argument exact?
That makes a minister in holy things
The joy of many, and the dread of more,
His name a theme for praise and for reproach?....
That, while it gives us worth in God's account,
Depreciates and undoes us in our own?
What pearl is it that rich men cannot buy,
That learning is too proud to gather up;
But which the poor, and the despis'd of all,
Seek and obtain, and often find unsought?
Tell me....and I will tell thee what is truth.

O, friendly to the best pursuits of man,
Friendly to thought, to virtue, and to peace,
Domestic life in rural leisure pass'd!
Few know thy value, and few taste thy sweets;
Though many boast thy favors, and affect
To understand and choose thee for their own.
But foolish man foregoes his proper bliss,
Ev'n as his first progenitor, and quits,
Though plac'd in paradise, (for earth has still
Some traces of her youthful beauty left)
Substantial happiness for transient joy.
Scenes form'd for contemplation, and to nurse

The growing seeds of wisdom ; that suggest,
By ev'ry pleasing image they present,
Reflections such as meliorate the heart,
Compose the passions, and exalt the mind ;
Scenes such as these 'tis his supreme delight
To fill with riot, and defile with blood.
Should some contagion, kind to the poor brutes
We persecute, annihilate the tribes
That draw the sportsman over hill and dale,
Fearless, and rapt away from all his cares ;
Should never game-fowl hatch her eggs again,
Nor baited hook deceive the fish's eye ;
Could pageantry and dance, and feast and song,
Be quell'd in all our summer-months' retreat ;
How many self-deluded nympths and swains,
Who dream they have a taste for fields and groves,
Would find them hideous nurs'ries of the spleen,
And crowd the roads, impatient for the town !
They love the country, and none else, who seek
For their own sake its silence and its shade..
Delights which who would leave, that has a heart
Susceptible of pity, or a mind
Cultur'd and capable of sober thought,
For all the savage din of the swift pack,
And clamors of the field ?....Detested sport,
That owes its pleasures to another's pain ;
That feeds upon the sobs and dying shrieks
Of harmless nature, dumb, but yet endu'd
With eloquence, that agonies inspire,
Of silent tears, and heart-distending sighs ?
Vain tears, alas, and sighs, that never find
A corresponding tone in jovial souls !

Well....one at least is safe.   One shelter'd hare
Has never heard the sanguinary yell
Of cruel man, exulting in her woes.
Innocent partner of my peaceful home,
Whom ten long years' experience of my care
Has made at last familiar; she has lost
Much of her vigilant instinctive dread,
Not needful here, beneath a roof like mine.
Yes....thou may'st eat thy bread, and lick the hand
That feeds thee; thou may'st frolic on the floor
At evening, and at night retire secure
To thy straw couch, and slumber unalarm'd;
For I have gain'd thy confidence, have pledg'd
All that is human in me to protect
Thine unsuspecting gratitude and love.
If I survive thee, I will dig thy grave;
And, when I place thee in it, sighing, say,
I knew at least one hare that had a friend.

    How various his employments, whom the world
Calls idle; and who justly, in return,
Esteems that busy world an idler too!
Friends, books, a garden, and perhaps his pen,
Delightful industry enjoy'd at home,
And nature in her cultivated trim
Dress'd to his taste, inviting him abroad....
Can he want occupation who has these?
Will he be idle who has much t' enjoy?
Me, therefore, studious of laborious ease,
Not slothful; happy to deceive the time,
Not waste it; and aware that human life
Is but a loan to be repaid with use,

When HE shall call his debtors to account
From whom are all our blessings; bus'ness finds
Ev'n here: while sedulous I seek t' improve,
At least neglect not, or leave unemploy'd,
The mind he gave me; driving it, though slack,
Too oft, and much impeded in its work,
By causes not to be divulg'd in vain,
To its just point....the service of mankind.
He that attends his interior self,
That has a heart, and keeps it; has a mind
That hungers, and supplies it; and who seeks
A social, not a dissipated life,
Has business; feels himself engag'd t' achieve
No unimportant, though a silent task.
A life all turbulence and noise, may seem,
To him that leads it, wise, and to be prais'd;
But wisdom is a pearl, with most success
Sought in still water, and beneath clear skies.
He that is ever occupied in storms,
Or dives not for it, or brings up instead,
Vainly industrious, a disgraceful prize.

  The morning finds the self-sequester'd man,
Fresh for his task, intend what task he may.
Whether inclement seasons recommend
His warm but simple home, where he enjoys,
With her who shares his pleasure and his heart,
Sweet converse, sipping calm the fragrant lymph
Which neatly she prepares; then to his book,
Well chosen, and not sullenly perus'd
In selfish silence, but imparted oft,
As ought occurs that she may smile to hear,

Or turn to nourishment, digested well.
Or, if the garden with its many cares,
All well repaid, demand him, he attends
The welcome call, conscious how much the hand
Of lubbard labor needs his watchful eye,
Oft loit'ring lazily, if not o'erseen,
Or misapplying his unskilful strength.
Nor does he govern only, or direct,
But much performs himself. No works indeed,
That ask robust tough sinews, bred to toil,
Servile employ; but such as may amuse,
Not tire, demanding rather skill than force.
Proud of his well-spread walls, he views his trees
That meet (no barren interval between)
With pleasure more than ev'n their fruits afford,
Which, save himself who trains them, none can feel.
These, therefore, are his own peculiar charge;
No meaner hand may discipline the shoots,
None but his steel approach them. What is weak,
Distemper'd, or has lost prolific pow'rs,
Impair'd by age, his unrelenting hand
Dooms to the knife: nor does he spare the soft
And succulent, that feeds its giant growth,
But barren, at th' expense of neighb'ring twigs
Less ostentatious, and yet studded thick
With hopeful gems. The rest, no portion left
That may disgrace his art, or disappoint
Large expectation, he disposes neat
At measur'd distances, that air and sun,
Admitted freely, may afford their aid,
And ventilate and warm the swelling buds.
Hence summer has her riches, autumn hence,

And hence ev'n winter fills his wither'd hand
With blushing fruits, and plenty, not his own.*
Fair recompence of labor well bestow'd,
And wise precaution; which a clime so rude
Makes needful still, whose spring is but the child
Of churlish winter, in her froward moods,
Discov'ring much the temper of her sire.
For oft, as if in her the stream of mild
Maternal nature had revers'd its course,
She brings her infants forth with many smiles;
But, once deliver'd, kills them with a frown.
He, therefore, timely warn'd, himself supplies
Her want of care, screening and keeping warm
The plenteous bloom, that no rough blast may sweep
His garlands from the boughs.   Again, as oft
As the sun peeps, and vernal airs breathe mild,
The fence withdrawn, he gives them ev'ry beam,
And spreads his hopes before the blaze of day.

    To raise the prickly and green-coated gourd,
So grateful to the palate, and when rare,
So coveted, else base and disesteem'd....
Food for the vulgar merely....is an art
That toiling ages have but just matur'd,
And at this moment unessay'd in song.
Yet gnats have had, and frogs and mice, long since,
Their eulogy; those sang the Mantuan bard,
And these the Grecian, in enobling strains;
And in thy numbers, Philips, shines for aye
The solitary shilling.   Pardon, then,
Ye sage dispensers of poetic fame,

    * Miraturque novos fructus et non sua poma....VIRG.
H

Th' ambition of one, meaner far, whose pow'rs,
Presuming an attempt not less sublime,
Pant for the praise of dressing to the taste
Of critic appetite, no sordid fare,
A cucumber, while costly yet and scarce.

The stable yields a stercoraceous heap,
Impregnated with quick fermenting salts,
And potent to resist the freezing blast:
For, ere the beech and elm have cast their leaf
Deciduous, when now November dark
Checks vegetation in the torpid plant,
Expos'd to his cold breath, the task begins.
Warily, therefore, and with prudent heed,
He seeks a favor'd spot; that where he builds
Th' agglomerated pile, his frame may front
The sun's meridian disk, and at the back
Enjoy close shelter, wall, or reeds, or hedge,
Impervious to the wind. First he bids spread
Dry fern or litter'd hay, that may imbibe
Th' ascending damps; then leisurely impose,
And lightly, shaking it with agile hand
From the full fork, the saturated straw.
What longest binds the closest, forms secure
The shapely side, that, as it rises, takes,
By just degrees, an overhanging breadth,
Shelt'ring the base with its projected eaves.
Th' uplifted frame, compact at ev'ry joint,
And overlaid with clear translucent glass,
He settles next upon the sloping mount,
Whose sharp declivity shoots off secure,
From the dash'd pane, the deluge as it falls.

He shuts it close, and the first labor ends.
Thrice must the voluble and restless earth
Spin round upon her axle, ere the warmth,
Slow gathering in the midst, through the square
   mass
Diffus'd, attain the surface : when, behold !
A pestilent and most corrosive steam,
Like a gross fog Bœotian, rising fast,
And fast condens'd upon the dewy sash,
Asks egress; which obtain'd, the overcharg'd
And drench'd conservatory breathes abroad,
In volumes wheeling slow, the vapor dank,
And, purified, rejoices to have lost
Its foul inhabitant.   But to assuage
Th' impatient fervor which it first conceives
Within its reeking bosom, threat'ning death
To his young hopes, requires discreet delay.
Experience, slow preceptress, teaching oft
The way to glory by miscarriage foul,
Must prompt him, and admonish how to catch
Th' auspicious moment, when the temper'd heat,
Friendly to vital motion, may afford
Soft fomentation, and invite the seed.
The seed, selected wisely, plump, and smooth,
And glossy, he commits to pots of size
Diminutive, well fill'd with well prepar'd
And fruitful soil, that has been treasur'd long,
And drank no moisture from the dripping clouds ;
These on the warm and genial earth, that hides
The smoking manure, and o'erspreads it all,
He places lightly, and, as time subdues
The rage of fermentation, plunges deep

In the soft medium, till they stand immers'd.
Then rise the tender germs, upstarting quick,
And spreading wide their spongy lobes; at first
Pale, wan, and lived; but assuming soon,
If fann'd by balmy and nutritious air,
Strain'd through the friendly mats, a vivid green.
Two leaves produc'd, two rough indented leaves,
Cautious, he pinches from the second stalk
A pimple, that portends a future sprout,
And interdicts its growth. Thence straight succeed
The branches, sturdy to his utmost wish,
Prolific all, and harbingers of more.
The crowded roots demand enlargement now,
And transplantation in an ampler space.
Indulg'd in what they wish, they soon supply
Large foliage, overshadowing golden flow'rs,
Blown on the summit of th' apparent fruit.
These have their sexes; and, when summer shines,
The bee transports the fertilizing meal
From flow'r to flow'r, and ev'n the breathing air
Wafts the rich prize to its appointed use.
Not so when winter scowls. Assistant art
Then acts in nature's office, brings to pass
The glad espousals, and ensures the crop.

Grudge not, ye rich, (since luxury must have
His dainties, and the world's more num'rous half
Lives by contriving delicates for you)
Grudge not the cost. Ye little know the cares,
The vigilance, the labor, and the skill,
That day and night are exercis'd, and hang
Upon the ticklish balance of suspense,

That ye may garnish your profuse regales,
With summer fruits, brought forth by wintry suns.
Ten thousand dangers lie in wait to thwart
The process.   Heat, and cold, and wind, and steam,
Moisture and drought, mice, worms, and swarming
        flies,
Minute as dust, and numberless, oft work
Dire disappointment that admits no cure,
And which no care can obviate.   It were long,
Too long, to tell th' expedients and the shifts,
Which he that fights a season so severe
Devises, while he guards his tender trust,
And oft, at last, in vain.   The learn'd and wise,
Sarcastic would exclaim, and judge the song
Cold as its theme, and like its theme, the fruit
Of too much labor, worthless when produc'd.

  Who loves a garden, loves a greenhouse too.
Unconscious of a less propitious clime,
There blooms exotic beauty, warm and snug,
While the winds whistle, and the snows descend,
The spiry myrtle, with unwith'ring leaf,
Shines there, and flourishes.   The golden boast
Of Portugal, and western India there,
The ruddier orange, and the paler lime,
Peep through their polish'd foliage at the storm,
And seem to smile at what they need not fear.
Th' amomum there with intermingling flow'rs,
And cherries, hangs her twigs.   Geranium boasts
Her crimson honors, and the spangled beau,
Ficoides, glitters bright the winter long.   ·
All plants, of ev'ry leaf, that can endure
     H 2

The winter's frown, if screen'd from his shrewd bite,
Live there, and prosper. Those Ausonia claims,
Levantine regions these; the Azores send
Their jessamine, her jessamine remote
Caffraria: foreigners from many lands,
They form one social shade, as if conven'd
By magic summons of th' Orphean lyre.
Yet just arrangement, rarely brought to pass,
But by a master's hand, disposing well
The gay diversities of leaf and flow'r,
Must lend its aid t' illustrate all their charms,
And dress the regular yet various scene.
Plant behind plant aspiring, in the van
The dwarfish, in the rear retir'd, but still
Sublime above the rest, the statelier stand.
So once were rang'd the sons of ancient Rome,
A noble show! while Roscius trod the stage;
And so, while Garrick, as renown'd as he,
The Sons of Albion; fearing each to lose
Some note of nature's music from his lips,
And covetous of Shakespeare's beauty, seen
In ev'ry flash of his fair-beaming eye.
Nor taste alone, and well-contriv'd display,
Suffice to give the marshall'd ranks the grace
Of their complete effect. Much yet remains
Unsung, and many cares are yet behind,
And more laborious; cares on which depend
Their vigor, injur'd soon, not soon restor'd.
The soil must be renew'd, which, often wash'd,
Loses its treasure of salubrious salts,
And disappoints the roots; the slender roots
Close interwoven, where they meet the vase,

Must smooth be shorn away ; the sapless branch
Must fly before the knife ; the wither'd leaf
Must be detach'd, and where it strews the floor
Swept with a woman's neatness, breeding else
Contagion, and disseminating death.
Discharge but these kind offices, (and who
Would spare, that loves them, offices like these ?)
Well they reward the toil.   The sight is pleas'd,
The scent regal'd, each odorif'rous leaf,
Each op'ning blossom, freely breathes abroad
Its gratitude, and thanks him with its sweets.

   So manifold, all pleasing in their kind,
All healthful, are th' employs of rural life,
Reiterated as the wheel of time
Runs round ; still ending, and beginning still.
Nor are these all.   To deck the shapely knoll,
That, softly swell'd and gaily dress'd, appears
A flow'ry island, from the dark green lawn
Emerging, must be deem'd a labor due
To no mean hand, and asks the touch of taste.
Here also, grateful mixture of well-match'd
And sorted hues, (each giving each relief,
And by contrasted beauty shining more)
Is needful.   Strength may wield the pond'rous spade,
May turn the clod, and wheel the compost home ;
But elegance, chief grace the garden shows,
And most attractive, is the fair result
Of thought, the creature of a polish'd mind.
Without it, all is Gothic as the scene
To which th' insipid citizen resorts,
Near yonder heath ; where industry mis-spent,

But proud of his uncouth ill-chosen task,
Has made a heav'n on earth; with suns and moons
Of close-ramm'd stones has charg'd th' encumber'd
  soil,
And fairly laid the zodiac in the dust.
He, therefore, who would see his flow'rs dispos'd
Sightly, and in just order, ere he gives
The beds the trusted treasure of their seeds,
Forecasts the future whole; that, when the scene
Shall break into its preconceiv'd display,
Each for itself, and all as with one voice
Conspiring, may attest his bright design.
Nor ev'n then, dismissing as performed,
His pleasant work, may he suppose it done.
Few self-supported flow'rs endure the wind,
Uninjur'd, but expect th' upholding aid
Of the smooth-shaven prop, and, neatly tied,
Are wedded thus, like beauty to old age,
For int'rest sake, the living to the dead.
Some clothe the soil that feeds them, far diffus'd,
And lowly creeping, modest, and yet fair,
Like virtue, thriving most where little seen :
Some, more aspiring, catch the neighbor shrub
With clasping tendrils, and invest his branch,
Else unadorn'd, with many a gay festoon,
And fragrant chaplet, recompensing well
The strength they borrow, with the grace they lend.
All hate the rank society of weeds,
Noisome, and ever greedy to exhaust
Th' impoverish'd earth; an over-bearing race,
That, like the multitude made faction mad,
Disturb good order, and degrade true worth.

Oh, blest seclusion from a jarring world,
Which he, thus occupied, enjoys! Retreat
Cannot indeed to guilty man restore
Lost innocence, or cancel follies past ;
But it has peace, and much secures the mind
From all assaults of evil ; proving still
A faithful barrier, not o'erleap'd with ease,
By vicious custom, raging uncontroll'd
Abroad, and desolating public life.
When fierce temptation, seconded within
By traitor appetite, and arm'd with darts
Temper'd in hell, invades the throbbing breast,
To combat may be glorious, and success
Perhaps may crown us; but to fly is safe.
Had I the choice of sublunary good,
What could I wish, that I possess not here ?
Health, leisure, means t' improve it, friendship,
        peace,
No loose or wanton, though a wand'ring, muse,
And constant occupation, without care.
Thus blest, I draw a picture of that bliss :
Hopeless, indeed, that dissipated minds,
And profligate abusers of a world,
Created fair so much in vain for them,
Should seek the guiltless joys that I describe,
Allur'd by my report : but sure no less,
That, self-condemn'd, they must neglect the prize,
And what they will not taste, must yet approve.
What we admire we praise ; and, when we praise,
Advance it into notice, that, its worth
Acknowledg'd, others may admire it too.
I therefore recommend, though at the risk

Of popular disgust, yet boldly still,
The cause of piety and sacred truth,
And virtue, and those scenes which God ordain'd
Should best secure them, and promote them most;
Scenes that I love, and with regret perceive
Forsaken, or through folly not enjoy'd.
(Pure is the nymph, though lib'ral of her smiles,
(And chaste, though unconfin'd, whom I extol.
Not as the prince in Shushan, when he call'd,
Vain-glorious of her charms, his Vashti forth,
To grace the full pavillion.   His design
Was but to boast his own peculiar good,
Which all might view with envy, none partake.
My charmer is not mine alone ; my sweets,
And she that sweetens all my bitters too,
Nature, enchanting nature, in whose form
And lineaments divine, I trace a hand
That errs not, and find raptures still renew'd,
Is free to all men....universal prize.
Strange, that so fair a creature should yet want
Admirers, and be destin'd to divide
With meaner objects, ev'n the few she finds !
Strip'd of her ornaments, her leaves and flow'rs,
She loses all her influence.   Cities then
Attract us, and neglected nature pines,
Abandon'd, as unworthy of our love.
But are not wholesome airs, though unperfum'd
By roses ; and clear suns, though scarcely felt ;
And groves, if unharmonious, yet secure
From clamor, and whose very silence charms;
To be prefer'd to smoke, to the eclipse
That Metropolitan volcanoes make,

Whose Stygian throats breathe darkness all day long.
And to the stir of commerce, driving slow,
And thund'ring loud, with his ten thousand wheels?
They would be, were not madness in the head,
And folly in the heart; were England now,
What England was, plain, hospitable, kind,
And undebauch'd.   But we have bid farewel
To all the virtues of those better days,
And all their honest pleasures.   Mansions once
Knew their own masters; and laborious hinds,
Who had surviv'd the father, serv'd the son.
Now the legitimate and rightful lord,
Is but a transient guest, newly arriv'd,
And soon to be supplanted.   He that saw
His patrimonial timber cast its leaf,
Sells the last scantling, and tranfers the price
To some shrewd sharper, ere it buds again.
Estates are landscapes, gaz'd upon a while,
Then advertiz'd, and auctioneer'd away.
The country starves, and they that feed th' o'er-
          charg'd
And surfeited lewd town with her fair dues,
By a just judgment, strip and starve themselves.
The wings that waft our riches out of sight,
Grow on the gamester's elbows; and th' alert
And nimble motion of those restless joints,
That never tire, soon fans them all away.
Improvement, too, the idol of the age,
Is fed with many a victim.   Lo, he comes!
Th' omnipotent magician, Brown, appears!
Down falls the venerable pile, th' abode
Of our forefathers....a grave whisker'd race,

But tasteless. Springs a palace in its stead,
But in a distant spot; where, more expos'd,
It may enjoy th' advantage of the north,
And aguish east, till time shall have transform'd
Those naked acres to a shel'tring grove.
He speaks, the lake in front becomes a lawn;
Woods vanish, hills subside, and valleys rise;
And streams, as if created for his use,
Pursue the track of his directing wand;
Sinuous or straight, now rapid, and now slow,
Now murm'ring soft, now roaring in cascades....
Ev'n as he bids! Th' enraptur'd owner smiles.
'Tis finish'd, and yet, finish'd as it seems,
Still wants a grace, the loveliest it could show,
A mine to satisfy th' enormous cost.
Drain'd to the last poor item of his wealth,
He sighs, departs, and leaves th' accomplish'd plan
That he has touch'd, retouch'd, many a long day
Labor'd, and many a night pursu'd in dreams,
Just when it meets his hopes, and proves the heav'n
He wanted, for a wealthier to enjoy!
And now perhaps the glorious hour is come,
When, having no stake left, no pledge t' endear
Her int'rests, or that gives her sacred cause
A moment's operation on his love,
He burns with most intense and flagrant zeal
To serve his country.   Ministerial grace,
Deals him out money from the public chest;
Or, if that mine be shut, some private purse
Supplies his need with an usurious loan,
To be refunded duly, when his vote,
Well-manag'd, shall have earn'd its worthy price.

Oh innocent, compar'd with arts like these,
Crape, and cock'd pistol, and the whistling ball
Sent through the trav'llers temples ! He that finds
One drop of Heav'n's sweet mercy in his cup,
Can dig, beg, rot, and perish, well content,
So he may wrap himself in honest rags,
At his last gasp ; but could not for a world,
Fish up his dirty and dependent bread,
From pools and ditches of the commonwealth,
Sordid and sick'ning at his own success.

   Ambition, av'rice, penury incurr'd
By endless riot, vanity, the lust
Of pleasure and variety, dispatch,
As duly as the swallows disappear,
The world of wand'ring knights and squires to town.
London ingulphs them all ! The shark is there,
And the shark's prey ; the spendthrift, and the leech
That sucks him.   There the sycophant, and he,
Who, with bare-headed and obsequious bows,
Begs a warm office, doom'd to a cold jail,
And groat per diem, if his patron frown.
The levee swarms, as if, in golden pomp,
Were character'd on ev'ry statesman's door,
"*Batter'd and bankrupt fortunes mended here.*"
These are the charms that sully and eclipse
The charms of nature.   'Tis the cruel gripe,
That lean hard-handed poverty inflicts,
The hope of better things, the chance to win,
The wish to shine, the thirst to be amus'd,
That at the sound of winter's hoary wing,
Unpeople all our countries, of such herds,

I

Of flutt'ring, loit'ring, cringing, begging, loose,
And wanton vagrants, as make London, vast
And boundless as it is, a crowded coop.

Oh thou resort and mart of all the earth,
Chequer'd with all complexions of mankind,
And spotted with all crimes; in whom I see
Much that I love, and more that I admire,
And all that I abhor; thou freckl'd fair,
That pleasest, and yet shock'st me, I can laugh,
And I can weep, can hope, and can despond,
Feel wrath, and pity, when I think on thee!
Ten righteous would have sav'd a city once,
And thou hast many righteous....Well for thee....
That salt preserves thee; more corrupted else,
And therefore more obnoxious, at this hour,
Than Sodom, in her day, had pow'r to be,
For whom God heard his Ab'ram plead in vain.

THE TASK,

A POEM.

BOOK IV.

ARGUMENT OF THE FOURTH BOOK.

The post comes in....The news-paper is read....The world contemplated at a distance....Address to winter....The rural amusements of a winter evening compared with the fashionable ones....Address to evening....A brown study....Fall of snow in the evening....The waggoner....A poor family piece....The rural thief....Public houses....The multitude of them censured....The farmer's daughter: what she was....what she is....The simplicity of country manners almost lost....Causes of the change....Desertion of the country by the rich....Neglect of magistrates....The militia principally in fault....The new recruit, and his transformation....Reflection on bodies corporate....The love of rural objects natural to all, and never to be totally extinguished.

THE TASK.

BOOK IV.

THE WINTER EVENING.

Hark! 'tis the twanging horn o'er yonder bridge,
That with its wearisome, but needful length,
Bestrides the wintry flood, in which the moon
Sees her unwrinkled face reflected bright;
He comes, the herald of a noisy world,
With spatter'd boots, strapp'd waist, and frozen
　　　locks;
News from all nations lumb'ring at his back.
True to his charge, the close-pack'd load behind,
Yet careless what he brings, his one concern
Is to conduct it to its destin'd inn,
And, having dropp'd the expected bag, pass on.
He whistles as he goes, light-hearted wretch,
Cold and yet cheerful: messenger of grief
Perhaps to thousands, and of joy to some;
To him indiff'rent, whether grief or joy.
Houses in ashes, and the fall of stocks,
Births, deaths, and marriages, epistles wet
With tears, that trickled down the writer's cheeks,
Fast as the periods from his fluent quill,
Or charg'd with am'rous sighs of absent swains,

1 2

Or Nymphs responsive, equally affect
His horse and him, unconscious of them all.
But oh the important budget! usher'd in
With such heart-shaking music, who can say
What are its tidings? have our troops awak'd?
Or do they still, as if with opium drugg'd,
Snore to the murmurs of th' Atlantic wave?
Is India free? and does she wear her plum'd
And jewell'd turban with the smile of peace?
Or do we grind her still? The grand debate,
The popular harrangue, the tart reply,
The logic, and the wisdom, and the wit,
And the loud laugh....I long to know them all;
I burn to set th' imprison'd wranglers free,
And give them voice and utt'rance once again.

Now stir the fire, and close the shutters fast,
Let fall the curtains, wheel the sofa round,
And, while the bubbling and loud-hissing urn
Throws up a steamy column, and the cups,
That cheer, but not inebriate, wait on each;
So let us welcome peaceful ev'ning in.
Not such his ev'ning, who with shining face,
Sweats in the crowded theatre, and squeez'd,
And bor'd, with elbow-points, through both his sides,
Out-scolds the ranting actor on the stage:
Nor his, who patient stands till his feet throb,
And his head thumps, to feed upon the breath
Of patriots, bursting with heroic rage,
Or placemen, all tranquility and smiles.
This folio of four pages, happy work!
Which not ev'n critics criticise; that holds

Inquisitive attention, while I read,
Fast bound in chains of silence, which the fair,
Though eloquent themselves, yet fear to break;
What is it, but a map of busy life,
Its fluctuations, and its vast concerns?
Here runs the mountainous and craggy ridge
That tempts ambition.   On the summit, see,
The seals of office glitter in his eyes;
He climbs, he pants, he grasps them! At his heels,
Close at his heels, a demagogue ascends,
And with a dex'trous jerk, soon twists him down,
And wins them, but to lose them in his turn.
Here rills of oily eloquence in soft
Meanders, lubricate the course they take;
The modest speaker is asham'd and griev'd
T' ingross a moment's notice, and yet begs,
Begs a propitious ear for his poor thoughts,
However trivial, all that he conceives.
Sweet bashfulness! it claims at least this praise;
The dearth of information, and good sense,
That it foretels us, always comes to pass.
Cat'racts of declamation thunder here;
There forests of no meaning spread the page,
In which all comprehension wanders, lost;
While fields of pleasantry amuse us there,
With merry descants on a nation's woes.
The rest appears a wilderness of strange,
But gay confusion; roses for the cheeks,
And lilies for the brows of faded age,
Teeth for the toothless, ringlets for the bald,
Heav'n, earth, and ocean, plunder'd of their sweets,
Nectareous essences, Olympian dews,

Sermons, and city feasts, and fav'rite airs,
Ethereal journies, submarine exploits,
And Katterfelto, with his hair on end,
At his own wonders, wond'ring for his bread.

   'Tis pleasant, through the loop-holes of retreat,
To peep at such a world; to see the stir
Of the great Babel, and not feel the crowd;
To hear the roar she sends through all her gates,
At a safe distance, where the dying sound
Falls a soft murmur on th' uninjur'd ear.
Thus sitting, and surveying thus at ease,
The globe and its concerns, I seem advanc'd
To some secure, and more than mortal height,
That lib'rates and exempts me from them all.
It turns, submitted to my view, turns round,
With all its generations; I behold
The tumult, and am still. The sound of war
Has lost its terrors, ere it reaches me;
Grieves, but alarms me not. I mourn the pride
And av'rice that make man a wolf to man;
Hear the faint echo of those brazen throats,
By which he speaks the language of his heart,.
And sigh, but never tremble at the sound.
He travels and expatiates, as the bee,
From flow'r to flow'r, so he from land to land;
The manners, customs, policy of all,
Pay contribution to the store he gleans;
He sucks intelligence in ev'ry clime,
And spreads the honey of his deep research
At his return....a rich repast for me.
He travels, and I too. I tread his dock,

Ascend his topmast, through his peering eyes
Discover countries, with a kindred heart,
Suffer his woes, and share in his escapes;
While fancy, like the finger of a clock,
Runs the great circuit, and is still at home.

Oh Winter! ruler of th' inverted year,
Thy scatter'd hair, with sleet like ashes fill'd,
Thy breath congeal'd upon thy lips, thy cheeks
Fring'd with a beard, made white with other snows
Than those of age; thy forehead wrapt in clouds,
A leafless branch thy sceptre, and thy throne,
A sliding car, indebted to no wheels,
But urg'd by storms along its slipp'ry way,
I love thee, all unlovely as thou seem'st,
And dreaded as thou art! Thou hold'st the sun
A pris'ner in the yet undawning east,
Short'ning his journey between morn and noon,
And hurrying him, impatient of his stay,
Down to the rosy west; but kindly, still
Compensating his loss with added hours
Of social converse, and instructive ease,
And gath'ring, at short notice, in one group,
The family dispers'd, and fixing thought,
Not less dispers'd by day light and its cares.
I crown thee king of intimate delights,
Fire-side enjoyments, home-born happiness,
And all the comforts that the lowly roof
Of undisturb'd retirement, and the hours
Of long uninterrupted ev'ning, know.
No rattling wheels stop short before these gates;
No powder'd pert proficient in the art

Of sounding an alarm, assaults these doors
Till the street rings; no stationary steeds
Cough their own knell, while, heedless of the soun(
The silent circle fan themselves, and quake:
But here the needle plies its busy task,
The pattern grows, the well depicted flow'r,
Wrought patiently into the snowy lawn,
Unfolds its bosom; buds, and leaves, and sprigs,
And curling tendrils, gracefully dispos'd,
Follow the nimble finger of the fair;
A wreath that cannot fade, of flow'rs that blow
With most success, when all besides decay.
The poet's or historian's page, by one
Made vocal for th' amusement of the rest;
The sprightly lyre, whose treasure of sweet sound(
The touch, from many a trembling chord shakes out
And the clear voice, symphonious, yet distinct,
And in the charming strife triumphant still;
Beguile the night, and set a keener edge
On female industry; the threaded steel
Flies swiftly, and, unfelt, the task proceeds.
The volume clos'd, the customary rites
Of the last meal commence. A Roman meal;
Such as the mistress of the world once found
Delicious, when her patriots of high note,
Perhaps by moon-light, at their humble doors,
And under an old oak's domestic shade,
Enjoy'd....spare feast! a radish and an egg!
Discourse ensues, not trivial, yet not dull,
Nor such as with a frown, forbids the play
Of fancy, or proscribes the sound of mirth:
Nor do we madly, like an impious world,

Who deem religion frenzy, and the God
That made them, an intruder on their joys,
Start at his awful name, or deem his praise
A jarring note. Themes of a graver tone,
Exciting oft our gratitude and love,
While we retrace, with mem'ry's pointing wand,
That calls the past to our exact review,
The dangers we have 'scap'd, the broken snare,
The disappointed foe, deliv'rance found
Unlook'd for, life preserv'd and peace restor'd....
Fruits of omnipotent eternal love.
Oh ev'nings, worthy of the gods! exclaim'd
The Sabine bard. Oh ev'nings, I reply,
More to be priz'd and coveted than yours,
As more illum'd, and with nobler truths,
That I and mine, and those we love, enjoy.

   Is winter hideous in a garb like this?
Needs he the tragic fur, the smoke of lamps,
The pent-up breath of an unsav'ry throng,
To thaw him into feeling; or the smart
And snappish dialogue, that flippant wits
Call comedy, to prompt him with a smile?
The self-complacent actor, when he views
(Stealing a side-long glance at a full house)
The slope of faces, from the floor to th' roof,
(As if one master-spring control'd them all)
Relax'd into an universal grin,
Sees not a count'nance there that speaks a joy,
Half so refin'd, or so sincere as ours.
Cards were superfluous here, with all the tricks
That idleness has ever yet contriv'd,

To fill the void of an unfurnish'd brain,
To palliate dulness, and give time a shove.
Time, as he passes us, has a dove's wing,
Unsoil'd, and swift, and of a silken sound ;
But the world's time, is time in masquerade!
Theirs, should I paint him, has his pinions fledg'd
With motley plumes ; and where the peacock shows
His azure eyes, is tinctur'd black and red,
With spots quadrangular, of di'mond form,
Ensanguin'd hearts, clubs typical of strife,
And spades, the emblem of untimely graves.
What should be, and what was, an hour-glass once,
Becomes a dice-box, and a billiard mast
Well does the work of his destructive scythe.
Thus deck'd, he charms a world, whom fashion blinds
To his true worth, most pleas'd, when idle most ;
Whose only happy, are their wasted hours.
Ev'n misses, at whose age their mothers wore
The back-string and the bib, assume the dress
Of womanhood, sit pupils in the school
Of card-devoted time, and, night by night,
Plac'd at some vacant corner of the board,
Learn ev'ry trick, and soon play all the game.
But truce with censure.   Roving, as I rove,
Where shall I find an end, or how proceed ?
As he that travels far, oft turns aside,
To view some rugged rock, or mould'ring tow'r,
Which seen, delights him not ; then, coming home,
Describes and prints it, that the world may know
How far he went for what was nothing worth ;
So I, with brush in hand, and pallet spread,
With colours mix'd for a far diff'rent use,

Paint cards, and dolls, and ev'ry idle thing,
That fancy finds in her excursive flights.

  Come, Ev'ning, once again, season of peace;
Return, sweet Ev'ning, and continue long!
Methinks I see thee in the streaky west,
 With matron-step, slow-moving, while the night
Treads on thy sweeping train; one hand employ'd
In letting fall the curtain of repose
On bird and beast, the other charg'd for man,
With sweet oblivion of the cares of day:
Not sumptuously adorn'd, nor needing aid,
Like homely featur'd night, of clust'ring gems;
A star or two, just twinkling on thy brow,
Suffices thee; save, that the moon is thine
No less than hers, not worn indeed on high,
With ostentatious pageantry, but set
With modest grandeur, in thy purple zone,
Resplendent less, but of an ampler round.
Come then, and thou shalt find thy vot'ry calm,
Or make him so.   Composure is thy gift;
And, whether I devote thy gentle hours
To books, to music, or the poet's toil;
To weaving nets for bird-alluring fruit;
Or twining silken threads round iv'ry reels,
 When they command, whom man was born to please;
I slight thee not, but make thee welcome still.

  Just when our drawing-rooms begin to blaze
With lights, by clear reflection multiplied
From many a mirror, in which he of Gath,
Goliah, might have seen his mighty bulk
                 x

Whole, without stooping, tow'ring crest and all,
My pleasures, too, begin. But me, perhaps,
The glowing hearth may satisfy a while
With faint illumination, that uplifts
The shadow to the ceiling, there by fits
Dancing uncouthly to the quiv'ring flame.
Not undelightful is an hour to me
So spent in parlor twilight : such a gloom
Suits well the thoughtful, or unthinking mind,
The mind contemplative, with some new theme
Pregnant, or indispos'd alike to all.
Laugh ye, who boast your more mercurial pow'rs,
That never feel a stupor, know no pause,
Nor need one : I am conscious, and confess,
Fearless, a soul that does not always think.
Me oft has fancy, ludicrous and wild,
Sooth'd with a waking dream of houses, tow'rs,
Trees, churches, and strange visages, express'd
In the red cinders, while with poring eye
I gaz'd, myself creating what I saw.
Nor less amus'd have I, quiescent, watch'd
The sooty films that play upon the bars,
Pendulous, and foreboding, in the view
Of superstition, prophesying still,
Though still deceiv'd, some stranger's near ap-
      proach.
'Tis thus the understanding takes repose,
In indolent vacuity of thought,
And sleeps and is refresh'd. Meanwhile the face
Conceals the mood lethargic, with a mask
Of deep deliberation, as the man
Were task'd to his full strength, absorb'd and lost.

Thus oft, reclin'd at ease, I lose an hour
At ev'ning, till at length the freezing blast,
That sweeps the bolted shutter, summons home
The recollected pow'rs ; and, snapping short
The glassy threads, with which the fancy weaves
Her brittle toys, restores me to myself.
How calm is my recess; and how the frost,
Raging abroad, and the rough wind, endear
The silence and the warmth, enjoy'd within !
I saw the woods and fields, at close of day,
A variegated show ; the meadows green,
Though faded ; and the lands, where lately wav'd
The golden harvest, of a mellow brown,
Upturn'd so lately by the forceful share.
I saw far off the weedy fallows smile
With verdure, not unprofitable, graz'd
By flocks, fast feeding, and selecting each
His fav'rite herb ; while all the leafless groves,
That skirt th' horizon, wore a sable hue,
Scarce notic'd, in the kindred dusk of eve.
To-morrow brings a change, a total change !
Which even now, though silently perform'd,
And slowly, and by most unfelt, the face
Of universal nature undergoes.
Fast falls a fleecy show'r : the downy flakes,
Descending, and with never-ceasing lapse,
Softly alighting upon all below,
Assimulate all objects.   Earth receives,
Gladly, the thick'ning mantle ; and the green
And tender blade, that fear'd the chilling blast,
Escapes unhurt beneath so warm a veil.

In such a world ; so thorny, and where none
Finds happiness unblighted ; or, if found,
Without some thistly sorrow at its side ;
It seems the part of wisdom, and no sin
Against the law of love, to measure lots
With less distinguish'd than ourselves ; that thus,
We may with patience, bear our mod'rate ills,
And sympathise with others, suff'ring more.
Ill fares the trav'ller now, and he that stalks
In pond'rous boots, beside his reeking team.
The wain goes heavily, impeded sore
By congregated loads, adhering close
To the clogg'd wheels ; and in its sluggish pace,
Noiseless, appears a moving hill of snow.
The toiling steeds expand the nostril wide,
While ev'ry breath, by respiration strong,
Forc'd downward, is consolidated soon
Upon their jutting chests.   He, form'd to bear
The pelting brunt of the tempestuous night,
With half-shut eyes, and pucker'd cheeks, and teeth
Presented bare against the storm, plods on.
One hand secures his hat, save when with both
He brandishes his pliant length of whip,
Resounding oft, and never heard in vain.
Oh happy ; and, in my account, denied
That sensibility of pain, with which
Refinement is endued, thrice happy thou !
Thy frame, robust and hardy, feels indeed
The piercing cold, but feels it unimpair'd.
The learned finger never need explore
Thy vig'rous pulse ; and the unhealthful east,
That breathes the spleen, and searches ev'ry bone

Of the infirm, is wholesome air to thee.
Thy days roll on, exempt from household care ;
Thy waggon is thy wife ; and the poor beasts,
That drag the dull companion to and fro,
Thine helpless charge, dependent on thy care.
Ah, treat them kindly ! rude as thou appears't,
Yet show that thou hast mercy ! which the great,
With needless hurry, whirl'd from place to place,
Humane as they would seem, not always show.

Poor, yet industrious, modest, quiet, neat ;
Such claim compassion in a night like this,
And have a friend in ev'ry feeling heart.
Warm'd, while it lasts, by labor, all day long
They brave the season, and yet find at eve,
Ill clad and fed but sparely, time to cool.
The frugal housewife trembles when she lights
Her scanty stock of brush-wood, blazing clear,
But dying soon, like all terrestrial joys.
The few small embers left, she nurses well ;
And, while her infant race, with outspread hands,
And crowded knees, set cow'ring o'er the sparks,
Retires, content to quake, so they be warm'd.
The man feels least, as more inur'd than she
To winter, and the current in his veins
More briskly mov'd by his severer toil ;
Yet he, too, finds his own distress in theirs.
The taper soon extinguish'd, which I saw
Dangled along at the cold finger's end
Just when the day declin'd, and the brown loaf
Lodg'd on the shelf, half eaten, without sauce.
Of sav'ry cheese, or butter, costlier still ;

Sleep seems their only refuge ; for, alas,
Where penury is felt, the thought is chain'd,
And sweet coloquial pleasures are but few !
With all this thrift, they thrive not.   All the care
Ingenious parsimony takes, but just
Saves the small inventory, bed, and stool,
Skillet, and old carv'd chest, from public sale.
They live, and live without extorted alms,
From grudging hands ; but other boasts have none,
To sooth their honest pride, that scorns to beg,
Nor comfort else, but in their mutual love.
I praise you much, ye meek and patient pair,
For ye are worthy ; choosing rather far
A dry, but independent crust, hard earn'd,
And eaten with a sigh, than to endure
The rugged frowns, and insolent rebuffs
Of knaves in office, partial in the work
Of distribution ; lib'ral of their aid
To clam'rous importunity in rags,
But oft times deaf to suppliants, who would blush
To wear a tatter'd garb, however coarse,
Whom famine cannot reconcile to filth :
These ask with painful shyness, and, refus'd,
Because deserving, silently retire !
But be ye of good courage ! Time itself
Shall much befriend you. Time shall give increase ;
And all your num'rous progeny, well train'd,
But helpless, in few years shall find their hands,
And labor too. Meanwhile ye shall not want,
What, conscious of your virtues, we can spare,
Nor what a wealthier than ourselves may send.

I mean the man, who, when the distant poor
Need help, denies them nothing but his name.

But poverty, with most, who whimper forth
Their long complaints, is self-inflicted woe;
Th' effect of laziness, or sottish waste.
Now goes the nightly thief prowling abroad
For plunder; much solicitous how best
He may compensate for a day of sloth,
By works of darkness, and nocturnal wrong.
Woe to the gard'ner's pale, the farmer's hedge,
Plash'd neatly, and secur'd with driven stakes,
Deep in the loamy bank.   Uptorn by strength,
Resistless in so bad a cause, but lame
To better deeds, he bundles up the spoil....
An ass's burthen....and, when laden most,
And heaviest, light of foot, steals fast away.
Nor does the boarded hovel better guard
The well-stack'd pile of riven logs and roots
From his pernicious force.   Nor will he leave
Unwrench'd the door, however well secur'd,
Where Chanicleer, amidst his haram sleeps
In unsuspecting pomp.   Twitch'd from the perch,
He gives the princely bird, with all his wives,
To his voracious bag, struggling in vain,
And loudly wond'ring at the sudden change.
Nor this to feed his own! 'Twere some excuse,
Did pity of their suff'rings, warp aside
His principle, and tempt him into sin
For their support, so destitute....But they,
Neglected, pine at home; themselves, as more
Expos'd than others, with less scruple made

His victims, robb'd of their defenceless all.
Cruel is all he does. 'Tis quenchless thirst
Of ruinous ebriety, that prompts
His ev'ry action, and imbrutes the man.
Oh for a law, to noose the villain's neck,
Who starves his own; who persecutes the blood
He gave them in his children's veins; and hates
And wrongs the woman, he has sworn to love!

    Pass where we may, through city, or through town,
Village, or hamlet, of this merry land,
Though lean and beggar'd, ev'ry twentieth pace,
Conducts th' unguarded nose to such a whiff
Of stale debauch, forth-issuing from the styes
That law has licens'd, as makes temp'rance reel.
There sit, involv'd and lost in curling clouds
Of Indian fume, and guzzling deep, the boor,
The lacquey, and the groom: the craftsman there,
Takes a Lethæan leave of all his toil;
Smith, cobbler, joiner, he that plies the shears,
And he that kneeds the dough; all loud alike,
All learned, and all drunk! The fiddle screams,
Plaintive and piteous, as it wept and wail'd
Its wasted tones and harmony unheard:
Fierce the dispute, whate'er the theme; while she,
Fell Discord, arbitress of such debate,
Perch'd on the sign-post, holds with even hand
Her undecisive scales. In this she lays
A weight of ignorance; in that of pride;
And smiles, delighted with th' eternal poise.
Dire is the frequent curse, and its twin sound,
The cheek-distending oath, not to be prais'd

As ornamental, musical, polite,
Like those which modern senators employ,
Whose oath is rhet'ric, and who swear for fame!
Behold the schools in which plebeian minds,
Once simple, are initiated in arts,
Which some may practise with politer grace,
But none with readier skill !.....'tis here they learn
The road that leads, from competence and peace,
To indigence and rapine ; till at last,
Society, grown weary of the load,
Shakes her encumber'd lap, and casts them out.
But censure profits little : vain th' attempt
To advertise in verse a public pest,
That, like the filth with which the peasant feeds
His hungry acres, stinks, and is of use.
Th' excise is fatten'd with the rich result
Of all this riot; and ten thousand casks,
Forever dribbling out their base contents,
Touch'd by the Midas finger of the state,
Bleed gold for ministers to sport away.
Drink, and be mad, then ; 'tis your country bids!
Gloriously drunk, obey th' important call !
Her cause demands th' assistance of your throats ;...
Ye all can swallow, and she asks no more.

　　Would I had fall'n upon those happier days
That poets celebrate ; those golden times,
And those Arcadian scenes, that Maro sings,
And Sidney, warbler of poetic prose.
Nymphs were Dianas then, and swains had hearts
That felt their virtues ; innocence, it seems,
From courts dismiss'd, found shelter in the groves ;

The foot-steps of simplicity, impress'd
Upon the yielding herbage, (so they sing)
Then were not all effac'd : then speech profane,
And manners profligate, were rarely found,
Observ'd as progidies, and soon reclaim'd.
Vain wish! those days were never; airy dreams
Sat for the picture ; and the poet's hand,
Imparting substance to an empty shade,
Impos'd a gay delirium for a truth.
Grant it :....I still must envy them an age
That favor'd such a dream, in days like these,
Impossible, when virtue is so scarce,
That to suppose a scene where she presides,
Is tramontane, and stumbles all belief.
No: we are polish'd now! The rural lass,
Whom once her virgin modesty and grace,
Her artless manners, and her neat attire,
So dignified, that she was hardly less
Than the fair shepherdess of old romance,
Is seen no more.   The character is lost!
Her head, adorn'd with lappets pinn'd aloft,
And ribbons streaming gay, superbly rais'd
And magnified beyond all human size,
Indebted to some smart wig-weaver's hand
For more than half the tresses it sustains;
Her elbows ruffled, and her tott'ring form,
Ill propp'd upon French heels ; she might be deem'd
(But that the basket dangling on her arm
Interprets her more truly) of a rank
Too proud for dairy work, or sale of eggs.
Expect her soon with foot-boy at her heels,

No longer blushing for her awkward load,
Her train, and her umbrella, all her care!

The town has ting'd the country; and the stain
Appears a spot upon a vestal's robe,
The worse for what it soils.   The fashion runs
Down into scenes still rural; but, alas!
Scenes rarely grac'd with rural manners now.
Time was, when, in the pastoral retreat,
Th' unguarded door was safe; men did not watch
T' invade another's right, or guard their own.
Then sleep was undisturb'd by fear, unscar'd
By drunken howlings; and the chilling tale
Of midnight murder, was a wonder heard
With doubtful credit, told to frighten babes.
But farewel now to unsuspicious nights,
And slumbers unalarm'd! Now, ere you sleep,
See that your polish'd arms be prim'd with care,
And drop the night-bolt; ruffians are abroad;
And the first larum of the cock's shrill throat
May prove a trumpet, summoning your ear
To horrid sounds of hostile feet within.
Ev'n day-light has its dangers; and the walk,
Through pathless wastes and woods, unconscious
          once
Of other tenants, than melodious birds
Or harmless flocks, is hazardous and bold.
Lamented change! to which full many a cause
Invet'rate, hopeless of a cure, conspires.
The course of human things from good to ill,
From ill to worse, is fatal, never fails.
Increase of pow'r begets increase of wealth;

Wealth luxury, and luxury excess ;
Excess, the scrofulous and itchy plague
That seizes first the opulent, descends
To the next rank contagious ; and in time,
Taints downward all the graduated scale
Of order, from the chariot to the plough.
The rich, and they that have an arm to check
The license of the lowest in degree,
Desert their office ; and themselves, intent
On pleasure, haunt the capital, and thus,
To all the violence of lawless hands,
Resign the scenes their presence might protect.
Authority herself not seldom sleeps,
Though resident, and witness of the wrong.
The plump convivial parson often bears
The magisterial sword in vain, and lays
His rev'rence and his worship, both to rest
On the same cushion of habitual sloth.
Perhaps timidity restrains his arm;
When he should strike he trembles, and sets free,
Himself enslav'd by terror of the band,
Th' audacious convict, whom he dares not bind.
Perhaps, though by profession ghostly pure,
He too may have his vice, and sometimes prove
Less dainty than becomes his grave outside
In lucrative concerns.   Examine well
His milk-white hand; the palm is hardly clean....
But here and there an ugly smutch appears.
Foh ! 'twas a bribe that left it : he has touch'd
Corruption ! Whoso seeks an audit here
Propitious, pays his tribute, game or fish,
Wild-fowl or ven'son ; and his errand speeds.

But faster far, and more than all the rest,
A noble cause, which none who bears a spark
Of public virtue, ever wish'd remov'd,
Works the deplor'd and mischievous effect.
'Tis universal soldiership has stabb'd
The heart of merit in the meaner class.
Arms, through the vanity and brainless rage
Of those that bear them, in whatever cause,
Seem most at variance with all moral good,
And incompatible with serious thought.
The clown, the child of nature, without guile,
Blest with an infant's ignorance of all
But his own simple pleasures; now and then
A wrestling-match, a foot-race, or a fair;
Is ballotted, and trembles at the news:
Sheepish he doffs his hat, and, mumbling, swears
A bible oath to be whate'er they please,
To do he knows not what! The task perform'd,
That instant he becomes the sergeant's care,
His pupil, and his torment, and his jest.
His awkward gait, his introverted toes,
Bent knees, round shoulders, and dejected looks,
Procure him many a curse. By slow degrees,
Unapt to learn, and form'd of stubborn stuff,
He yet by slow degrees puts off himself,
Grows conscious of a change, and likes it well:
He stands erect; his slouch becomes a walk;
He steps right onward, martial in his air,
His form, and movement; is as smart above
As meal and larded locks can make him; wears
His hat, or his plum'd helmet, with a grace;
And, his three years of heroship expir'd,

L

Returns indignant to the slighted plough.
He hates the field, in which no fife or drum
Attends him; drives his cattle to a march;
And sighs for the smart comrades he has left.
'Twere well if his exterior change were all....
But with his clumsy port the wretch has lost
His ignorance and harmless manners too!
To swear, to game, to drink; to show at home,
By lewdness, idleness, and sabbath-breach,
The great proficiency he made abroad;
T' astonish and to grieve his gazing friends;
To break some maiden's and his mother's heart;
To be a pest where he was useful once;
Are his sole aim, and all his glory, now!

Man in society is like a flow'r
Blown in its native bed: 'tis there alone
His faculties, expanded in full bloom,
Shine out; there only reach their proper use.
But man, associated and leagu'd with man
By regal warrant, or self-join'd by bond
For int'rest-sake, or swarming into clans
Beneath one head for purposes of war,
Like flow'rs selected from the rest, and bound
And bundled close to fill some crowded vase,
Fades rapidly, and, by compression marr'd,
Contracts defilement not to be endur'd.
Hence charter'd boroughs are such public plagues;
And burghers, men immaculate perhaps
In all their private functions, once combin'd,
Become a loathsome body; only fit
For dissolution, hurtful to the main.

Hence merchants, unimpeachable of sin
Against the charities of domestic life,
Incorporated, seem at once to lose
Their nature ; and, disclaiming all regard
For mercy and the common rights of man,
Build factories with blood, conducting trade
At the sword's point, and dying the white robe
Of innocent commercial justice, red.
Hence, too, the field of glory, as the world
Misdeems it, dazzled by its bright array,
With all its majesty of thund'ring pomp,
Enchanting music and immortal wreaths,
Is but a school where thoughtlessness is taught
On principle, where foppery atones
For folly, gallantry for every vice.

   But, slighted as it is, and by the great
Abandon'd, and, which still I more regret,
Infected with the manners and the modes
I knew not once, the country wins me still.
I never fram'd a wish, or form'd a plan,
That flatter'd me with hopes of earthly bliss,
But there I laid the scene.   There early stray'd
My fancy, ere yet liberty of choice
Had found me, or the hope of being free.
My very dreams were rural ; rural, too,
The first-born efforts of my youthful muse,
Sportive, and jingling her poetic bells
Ere yet her ear was mistress of their pow'rs.
No bard could please me but whose lyre was tun'd
To nature's praises.   Heroes and their feats
Fatigu'd me, never weary of the pipe

Of Tityrus, assembling, as he sang,
The rustic throng beneath his fav'rite beech.
Then Milton had indeed a poet's charms:
New to my taste, his Paradise surpass'd
The struggling efforts of my boyish tongue
To speak its excellence.   I danc'd for joy.
I marvel'd much, that, at so ripe an age
As twice seven years, his beauties had then first
Engag'd my wonder ; and, admiring still,
And still admiring, with regret suppos'd
The joy half lost because not sooner found.
There, too, enamor'd of the life I lov'd,
Pathetic in its praise, in its pursuit
Determin'd, and possessing it at last
With transports such as favor'd lovers feel,
I studied, priz'd, and wish'd that I had known,
Ingenious Cowley! and, though now reclaim'd
By modern lights from an erroneous taste,
I cannot but lament thy splendid wit
Entangled in the cobwebs of the schools.
I still revere thee, courtly though retir'd ;
Though stretch'd at ease in Chertsey's silent bow'rs,
Not unemploy'd ; and finding rich amends
For a lost world in solitude and verse.
'Tis born with all: the love of nature's works
Is an ingredient in the compound man,
Infus'd at the creation of the kind.
And, though the Almighty Maker has throughout
Discriminated each from each, by strokes
And touches of his hand, with so much art
Diversified, that two were never found
Twins at all points....yet this obtains in all, .

That all discern a beauty in his works,
And all can taste them: minds that have been form'd
And tutor'd, with a relish more exact,
But none without some relish, none unmov'd.
It is a flame that dies not even there,
Where nothing feeds it: neither business, crowds,
Nor habits of luxurious city-life;
Whatever else they smother of true worth
In human bosoms; quench it, or abate.
The villas with which London stands begirt,
Like a swarth Indian with his belt of beads,
Prove it.   A breath of unadult'rate air,
The glimpse of a green pasture, how they cheer
The citizen, and brace his languid frame!
Ev'n in the stifling bosom of the town,
A garden, in which nothing thrives, has charms
That soothe the rich possessor; much consol'd,
That here and there some sprigs of mournful mint,
Of nightshade, or valerian, grace the well
He cultivates   These serve him with a hint
That nature lives; that sight-refreshing green
Is still the liv'ry she delights to wear,
Though sickly samples of th' exub'rant whole.
What are the casements lin'd with creeping herbs,
The prouder sashes fronted with a range
Of orange, myrtle, or the fragrant weed,
The Frenchman's* darling? are they not all proofs,
That man, immur'd in cities, still retains
His inborn inextinguishable thirst
Of rural scenes, compensating his loss
By supplemental shifts, the best he may?
The most unfurnish'd with the means of life,

* Mignonette.

L 2

And they that never pass their brick-wall bounds
To range the fields and treat their lungs with air,
Yet feel the burning instinct: over-head
Suspend their crazy boxes, planted thick,
And water'd duly.   There the pitcher stands
A fragment, and the spoutless tea-pot there;
Sad witnesses how close-pent man regrets
The country, with what ardor he contrives
A peep at nature, when he can no more.

   Hail, therefore, patroness of health, and ease,
And contemplation, heart-consoling joys,
And harmless pleasures, in the throng'd abode
Of multitudes unknown! hail, rural life!
Address himself who will to the pursuit
Of honors, or emoluments, or fame;
I shall not add myself to such a chase,
Thwart his attempts, or envy his success.
Some must be great.   Great offices will have
Great talents.   And God gives to every man
The virtue, temper, understanding, taste,
That lifts him into life, and lets him fall
Just in the niche he was ordain'd to fill.
To the deliv'rer of an injur'd land
He gives a tongue t' enlarge upon, an heart
To feel, and courage to redress her wrongs;
To monarchs dignity; to judges sense;
To artists ingenuity and skill;
To me an unambitious mind, content
In the low vale of life, that early felt
A wish for ease and leisure, and ere long
Found here that leisure and that ease I wish'd.

THE TASK,

A POEM.

BOOK V.

ARGUMENT OF THE FIFTH BOOK.

A frosty morning....The foddering of cattle....The woodman and his dog....The poultry....Whimsical effects of frost at a water-fall....The Empress of Russia's palace of ice....Amusements of monarchs....War, one of them....Wars, whence....And whence monarchy....The evils of it....English and French loyalty contrast-ed....The Bastile, and a prisoner there....Liberty the chief recom-mendation of this country....Modern patriotism questionable, and why....The perishable nature of the best human institutions....Spiritual liberty not perishable....The slavish state of man by na-ture....Deliver him, Deist, if you can....Grace must do it....The respective merits of patriots and martyrs stated....Their different treatment....Happy freedom of the man whom grace makes free....His relish of the works of God....Address to the Creator.

THE TASK.

BOOK V.

THE WINTER MORNING WALK.

'T is morning; and the sun, with ruddy orb
Ascending, fires th' horizon; while the clouds,
That crowd away before the driving wind,
More ardent, as the disk imerges more,
Resembles most some city in a blaze,
Seen through the leafless wood. His slanting ray
Slides ineffectual down the snowy vale,
And, tinging all with his own rosy hue,
From ev'ry herb and ev'ry spiry blade,
Stretches a length of shadow o'er the field.
Mine, spindling into longitude immense,
In spite of gravity, and sage remark
That I myself am but a fleeting shade,
Provokes me to a smile. With eye askance,
I view the muscular proportion'd limb
Transform'd to a lean shank. The shapeless pair,
As they design'd to mock me, at my side
Take step for step; and, as I near approach
The cottage, walk along the plaster'd wall,
Prepost'rous sight! the legs without the man.
The verdure of the plain lies buried deep

Beneath the dazzling deluge : and the bents,
And coarser grass, upspearing o'er the rest,
Of late unsightly and unseen, now shine
Conspicuous, and, in bright apparel clad,
And fledg'd with icy feathers, nod superb.
The cattle mourn in corners, where the fence
Screens them, and seem half petrified to sleep
In unrecumbent sadness.   There they wait
Their wonted fodder; not like hung'ring man,
Fretful if unsupplied; but silent, meek,
And patient of the slow-pac'd swain's delay.
He from the stack carves out th' accustom'd load,
Deep plunging, and again deep plunging oft,
His broad keen knife into the solid mass:
Smooth as a wall the upright remnant stands,
With such undeviating and even force
He severs it away: no needless care,
Lest storms should overset the leaning pile
Deciduous, or its own unbalanc'd weight.
Forth goes the woodman, leaving unconcern'd
The cheerful haunts of man; to wield the axe
And drive the wedge, in yonder forest drear,
From morn to eve, his solitary task.
Shaggy, and lean, and shrewd, with pointed ears
And tail cropp'd short, half lurcher and half cur....
His dog attends him.   Close behind his heel
Now creeps he slow, and now with many a frisk,
Wide-scamp'ring, snatches up the drifted snow
With iv'ry teeth, or ploughs it with his snout:
Then shakes his powder'd coat, and barks for joy.
Heedless of all his pranks, the sturdy churl
Moves right toward the mark; nor stops for aught,

But now and then with pressure of his thumb
T' adjust the fragrant charge of a short tube
That fumes beneath his nose : the trailing cloud
Streams far behind him, scenting all the air.
Now from the roost, or from the neighb'ring pale,
Where, diligent to catch the first faint gleam
Of smiling day, they gossip'd side by side,
Come trooping at the housewife's well-known call,
The feather'd tribes domestic.   Half on wing,
And half on foot, they brush the fleecy flood,
Conscious and fearful of too deep a plunge.
The sparrows peep, and quit the shelt'ring eaves
To seize the fair occasion.   Well they eye
The scatter'd grain ; and, thievishly resolv'd
T' escape th' impending famine, often scar'd,
As oft return....a pert voracious kind.
Clean riddance quickly made, one only care
Remains to each....the search of sunny nook,
Or shed impervious to the blast.   Resign'd
To sad necessity, the cock foregoes
His wonted strut ; and, wading at their head
With well-consider'd steps, seems to resent
His alter'd gait and stateliness retrench'd.
How find the myriad, that in summer cheer
The hills and valleys with their ceaseless songs,
Due sustenance, or where subsist they now ?
Earth yields them nought : th' imprison'd worm is
          safe
Beneath the frozen clod ; all seeds of herbs
Lie cover'd close ; and berry-bearing thorns,
That feed the thrush, (whatever some suppose)
Afford the smaller minstrels no supply.

The long protracted rigor of the year
Thins all their numerous flocks. In chinks and holes
Ten thousand seek an unmolested end,
As instinct prompts; self-buried ere they die.
The very rooks and daws forsake the fields,
Where neither grub, nor root, nor earth-nut, now,
Repays their labor more; and, perch'd aloft
By the way-side, or stalking in the path,
Lean pensioners upon the trav'ller's track,
Pick up their nauseous dole, though sweet to them,
Of voided pulse, or half-digested grain.
The streams are lost amid the splendid blank,
O'erwhelming all distinction. On the flood,
Indurated and fix'd, the snowy weight
Lies undissolv'd; while silently beneath,
And unperceiv'd, the current steals away.
Not so, where, scornful of a check, it leaps
The mill-dam, dashes on the wrestless wheel,
And wantons in the pebbly gulph below:
No frost can bind it there; its utmost force
Can but arrest the light and smoky mist
That in its fall the liquid sheet throws wide.
And see, where it has hung th' embroider'd banks
With forms so various, that no pow'rs of art,
The pencil or the pen, may trace the scene!
Here glitt'ring turrets rise, upbearing high
(Fantastic misarrangement!) on the roof
Large growth of what may seem the sparkling trees
And shrubs of fairy land. The crystal drops
That trickle down the branches, fast congeal'd,
Shoot into pillars of pellucid length,
And prop the pile they but adorn'd before. . .

Here grotto within grotto safe defies
The sun-beam ; there, imboss'd and fretted wild,
The growing wonder takes a thousand shapes
Capricious, in which fancy seeks in vain
The likeness of some object seen before.
Thus nature works as if to mock at art,
And in defiance of her rival pow'rs ;
By these fortuitous and random strokes
Performing such inimitable feats
As she with all her rules can never reach.
Less worthy of applause, though more admir'd,
Because a novelty, the work of man,
Imperial mistress of the fur-clad Russ !
Thy most magnificent and mighty freak,
The wonder of the North.　No forest fell
When thou wouldst build ; no quarry sent its stores
T' enrich thy walls : but thou didst hew the floods,
And make thy marble of the glassy wave.
In such a palace Aristæus found
Cyrene, when he bore the plaintive tale
Of his lost bees to her maternal ear :
In such a palace, poetry might place
The armory of winter ; where his troops,
The gloomy clouds, find weapons, arrowy sleet,
Skin-piercing volley, blossom-bruising hail,
And snow that often blinds the trav'ller's course,
And wraps him in an unexpected tomb.
Silently as a dream the fabric rose ;....
No sound of hammer or of saw was there ;
Ice upon ice, the well adjusted parts
Were soon conjoin'd ; nor other cement ask'd
Than water interfus'd to make them one.

M

Lamps gracefully dispos'd, and of all hues,
Illumin'd ev'ry side: a wat'ry light
Gleam'd through the clear transparency, that seem'd
Another moon new risen, or meteor fall'n
From heav'n to earth, of lambent flame serene.
So stood the brittle prodigy; though smooth
And slipp'ry the materials, yet frost-bound
Firm as a rock. Nor wanted aught within,
That royal residence might well befit,
For grandeur or for use. Long wavy wreaths
Of flow'rs, that fear'd no enemy but warmth,
Blush'd on the pannels. Mirror needed none
Where all was vitreous; but in order due
Convivial table and commodious seat
(What seem'd at least commodious seat) were there;
Sofa, and couch, and high-built throne august.
The same lubricity was found in all,
And all was moist to the warm touch; a scene
Of evanescent glory, once a stream,
And soon to slide into a stream again.
Alas! 'twas but a mortifying stroke
Of undesign'd severity, that glanc'd
(Made by a monarch) on her own estate,
Of human grandeur and the courts of kings.
'Twas transient in its nature, as in show
'Twas durable; as worthless, as it seem'd
Intrinsically precious; to the foot
Treach'rous and false; it smil'd, and it was cold.

   Great princes have great playthings. Some have
      play'd
At hewing mountains into men, and some

At building human wonders mountain-high.
Some have amus'd the dull, sad years of life
(Life spent in indolence, and therefore sad)
With schemes of monumental fame; and sought
By pyramids and mausolean pomp,
Short-liv'd themselves, t' immortalize their bones.
Some seek diversion in the tented field,
And make the sorrows of mankind their sport.
But war's a game, which, were their subjects wise,
Kings would not play at.   Nations would do well
'T' extort their truncheons from the puny hands
Of heroes, whose infirm and baby minds
Are gratified with mischief; and who spoil,
Because men suffer it, their toy, the world.

    When Babel was confounded, and the great
Confed'racy of projectors, wild and vain,
Was split into diversity of tongues,
Then, as a shepherd separates his flock,
These to the upland, to the valley those,
God drave asunder, and assign'd their lot
To all the nations.   Ample was the boon
He gave them, in its distribution fair
And equal; and he bade them dwell in peace.
Peace was awhile their care; they plough'd, and
          sow'd,
And reap'd their plenty, without grudge or strife.
But violence can never longer sleep
Than human passions please.   In ev'ry heart
Are sown the sparks that kindle fiery war;
Occasion needs but fan them, and they blaze.
Cain had already shed a brother's blood:

The deluge wash'd it out; but left unquench'd
The seeds of murder in the breast of man.
Soon, by a righteous judgment, in the line
Of his descending progeny, was found
The first artificer of death; the shrewd
Contriver, who first sweated at the forge,
And forc'd the blunt and yet unbloodied steel
To a keen edge, and made it bright for war.
Him, Tubal nam'd, the Vulcan of old times,
The sword and falchion their inventor claim;
And the first smith was the first murd'rer's son.
His art surviv'd the waters; and ere long,
When man was multiplied and spread abroad
In tribes and clans, and had begun to call
These meadows and that range of hills his own,
The tasted sweets of property begat
Desire of more; and industry in some,
T' improve and cultivate their just demesne,
Made others covet what they saw so fair.
Thus war began on earth: these fought for spoil,
And those in self-defence.   Savage at first,
The onset, and irregular.   At length
One eminent above the rest, for strength,
For stratagem, or courage, or for all,
Was chosen leader: him they serv'd in war,
And him in peace, for sake of warlike deeds
Rev'renc'd no less.   Who could with him compare?
Or who so worthy to control themselves
As he whose prowess had subdu'd their foes?
Thus war, affording field for the display
Of virtue, made one chief, whom times of peace,
Which have their exigencies too, and call

For skill in government, at length made king.
King was a name too proud for man to wear
With modesty and meekness; and the crown,
So dazzling in their eyes who set it on,
Was sure t' intoxicate the brows it bound.
It is the abject property of most,
That, being parcel of the common mass,
And destitute of means to raise themselves,
They sink, and settle lower than they need.
They know not what it is to feel within
A comprehensive faculty, that grasps
Great purposes with ease, that turns and wields,
Almost without an effort, plans too vast
For their conception, which they cannot move.
Conscious of impotence, they soon grow drunk
With gazing, when they see an able man
Step forth to notice; and, besotted thus,
Build him a pedestal, and say, " Stand there,
" And be our admiration and our praise."
They roll themselves before him in the dust,
Then most deserving in their own account
When most extravagant in his applause
As if exalting him they rais'd themselves.
Thus by degrees, self-cheated of their sound
And sober judgment, that he is but man,
They demi-deify and fume him so,
That in due season he forgets it too.
Inflated and astrut with self-conceit,
He gulps the windy diet; and ere long,
Adopting their mistake, profoundly thinks
The world was made in vain, if not for him.
Thenceforth they are his cattle; drudges, born
                    M 2

To bear his burdens, drawing in his gears,
And sweating in his service, his caprice
Becomes the soul that animates them all.
He deems a thousand, or ten thousand lives,
Spent in the purchase of renown for him,
An easy reck'ning; and they think the same.
Thus kings were first invented, and thus kings
Were burnish'd into heroes, and became
The arbiters of this terraqueous swamp;
Storks among frogs, that have but croak'd and died.
Strange, that such folly as lifts bloated man
To eminence, fit only for a god,
Should ever drivel out of human lips,
Ev'n in the cradled weakness of the world!
Still stranger much, that, when at length mankind
Had reach'd the sinewy firmness of their youth,
And could discriminate and argue well
On subjects more mysterious, they were yet
Babes in the cause of freedom, and should fear
And quake before the gods themselves had made!
But above measure strange, that neither proof
Of sad experience, nor example set
By some whose patriot virtue has prevail'd,
Can, even now, when they are grown mature
In wisdom, and with philosophic deeps
Familiar, serve t' emancipate the rest!
Such dupes are men to custom, and so prone
To rev'rence what is ancient, and can plead
A course of long observance for its use,
That even servitude, the worst of ills,
Because deliver'd down from sire to son,
Is kept and guarded as a sacred thing!

But is it fit, or can it bear the shock
Of rational discussion, that a man,
Compounded and made up like other men,
Of elements tumultuous, in whom lust
And folly is as ample measure meet
As in the bosoms of the slaves he rules,
Should be a despot absolute, and boast
Himself the only freeman of his land ?
Should, when he pleases, and on whom he will,
Wage war, with any or with no pretence
Of provocation giv'n, or wrong sustain'd,
And force the beggarly last doit, by means
That his own humor dictates, from the clutch
Of poverty, that thus he may procure
His thousands, weary of penurious life,
A splendid opportunity to die ?
Say ye, (who, with less prudence than of old,
Jotham ascrib'd to his assembled trees
In politic convention) put your trust
I' th' shadows of a bramble, and, reclin'd
In fancied peace beneath his dang'rous branch,
Rejoice in him, and celebrate his sway,
Where find ye passive fortitude ? Whence springs
Your self-denying zeal, that holds it good
To stroke the prickly grievance, and to hang
His thorns with streamers of continual praise ?
We, too, are friends to loyalty.   We love
The king who loves the law, respects his bounds,
And reigns content within them : him we serve
Freely and with delight, who leaves us free :
But, recollecting still that he is man,
We trust him not too far. King though he be,

And king in England too, he may be weak,
And vain enough to be ambitious still;
May exercise amiss his proper pow'rs,
Or covet more than freemen choose to grant;
Beyond that mark is treason.   He is ours
T' administer, to guard, t' adorn the state,
But not to warp or change it.   We are his,
To serve him nobly in the common cause,
True to the death, but not to be his slaves.
Mark now the diff'rence, ye that boast your love
Of kings, between your loyalty and ours.
We love the man; the paltry pageant you.
We the chief patron of the commonwealth;
You the regardless author of its woes.
We, for the sake of liberty, a king;
You, chains and bondage, for a tyrant's sake.
Our love is principle, and has its root
In reason, is judicious, manly, free;
Your's, a blind instinct, crouches to the rod,
And licks the foot that treads it in the dust.
Were kingship as true treasure as it seems,
Sterling, and worthy of a wise man's wish,
I would not be a king to be belov'd
Causeless, and daub'd with undiscerning praise,
Where love is mere attachment to the throne,
Not to the man who fills it as he ought.

Whose freedom is by suff'rance, and at will
Of a superior, he is never free.
Who lives, and is not weary of a life
Expos'd to manacles, deserves them well.
The state that strives for liberty, though foil'd,

And forc'd t' abandon what she bravely sought,
Deserves at least applause for her attempt,
And pity for her loss.   But that's a cause
Not often unsuccessful : pow'r usurp'd
Is weakness when oppos'd ; conscious of wrong,
'Tis pusillanimous and prone to flight.
But slaves, that once conceive the glowing thought
Of freedom, in that hope itself possess
All that the contest calls for ; spirit, strength,
The scorn of danger, and united hearts ;
The surest presage of the good they seek.*

Then shame to manhood, and opprobrious more
To France than all her losses and defeats,
Old, or of later date, by sea or land,
Her house of bondage, worse than that of old
Which God aveng'd on Pharaoh....the Bastile !
Ye horrid tow'rs, th' abode of broken hearts ;
Ye dungeons ! and ye cages of despair !
That monarchs have supplied from age to age
With music such as suits their sov'reign ears !....
The sighs and groans of miserable men ;
There's not an English heart that would not leap
To hear that ye were fall'n at last ; to know
That ev'n our enemies, so oft employ'd
In forging chains for us, themselves were free.
For he who values liberty, confines
His zeal for her predominance within

* The Author hopes that he shall not be censured for unneces-
sary warmth upon so interesting a subject.   He is aware that it is
become almost fashionable to stigmatize such sentiments as no better than empty declamation ; but it is an ill symptom, and peculiar
to modern times.

No narrow bounds; her cause engages him
Wherever pleaded.   'Tis the cause of man.
There dwell the most forlorn of human kind;
Immur'd though unaccus'd, condemn'd untried,
Cruelly spar'd, and hopeless of escape!
There, like the visionary emblem seen
By him of Babylon, life stands a stump,
And, filletted about with hoops of brass,
Still lives, though all its pleasant boughs are gone.
To count the hour bell and expect no change;
And, ever, as the sullen sound is heard,
Still to reflect, that, though a joyless note
To him whose moments all have one dull pace,
Ten thousand rovers in the world at large
Account it music; that it summons some
To theatre, or jocund feast, or ball :
The wearied hireling finds it a release
From labor; and the lover, who has chid
Its long delay, feels ev'ry welcome stroke
Upon his heart-strings, trembling with delight....
To fly for refuge from distracting thought,
To such amusements as ingenious woe
Contrives, hard shifting, and without her tools....
To read engraven on the mouldy walls,
In stagg'ring types, his predecessor's tale,
A sad memorial, and subjoin his own....
To turn purveyor to an overgorg'd
And bloated spider, till the pamper'd pest
Is made familiar, watches his approach,
Comes at his call, and serves him for a friend....
To wear out time, in numbering to and fro
The studs that thick emboss his iron door;

Then downward and then upward, then aslant
And then alternate ; with a sickly hope
By dint of change to give his tasteless task
Some relish ; till the sum, exactly found
In all directions, he begins again....
Oh comfortless existence ! hemm'd around
With woes, which who that suffers would not kneel.
And beg for exile, or the pangs of death ?
That man should thus encroach on fellow man,
Abridge him of his just and native rights,
Eradicate him, tear him from his hold
Upon th' endearments of domestic life
And social, nip his fruitfulness and use,
And doom him for perhaps an heedless word
To barrenness, and solitude, and tears,
Moves indignation ; makes the name of king
(Of king whom such prerogative can please)
As dreadful as the Manichean god,
Ador'd through fear, strong only to destroy.

　　'Tis liberty alone that gives the flow'r
Of fleeting life its lustre and perfume ;
And we are weeds without it.   All constraint,
Except what wisdom lays on evil men,
Is evil ; hurts the faculties, impedes
Their progress in the road of science ; blinds
The eye-sight of discov'ry ; and begets,
In those that suffer it, a sordid mind
Bestial, a meagre intellect, unfit
To be the tenant of man's noble form.
Thee therefore still, blame-worthy as thou art,
With all thy loss of empire, and though squeez'd

By public exigence till annual food
Fails for the craving hunger of the state,
Thee I account still happy, and the chief
Among the nations, seeing thou art free :
My native nook of earth! Thy clime is rude,
Replete with vapors, and disposes much
All hearts to sadness, and none more than mine :
Thine unadult'rate manners are less soft
And plausible than social life requires,
And thou hast need of discipline and art
To give thee what politer France receives
From Nature's bounty....that humane address
And sweetness, without which no pleasure is
In converse, either starv'd by cold reserve,
Or flush'd with fierce dispute, a senseless brawl :
Yet, being free, I love thee : for the sake
Of that one feature, can be well content,
Disgrac'd as thou hast been, poor as thou art,
To seek no sublunary rest beside.
But, once enslav'd, farewell ! I could endure
Chains no where patiently ; and chains at home,
Where I am free by birth-right, not at all.
Then what were left of roughness in the grain
Of British natures, wanting its excuse
That it belongs to freemen, would disgust
And shock me. I should then, with double pain,
Feel all the rigor of thy fickle clime ;
And, if I must bewail the blessing lost,
For which our Hampdens and our Sidneys bled,
I would at least bewail it under skies
Milder, among a people less austere ;
In scenes, which, having never known me free,

Would not reproach me with the loss I felt.
Do I forebode impossible events,
And tremble at vain dreams? Heav'n grant I may!
But th' age of virtuous politics is past,
And we are deep in that of cold pretence.
Patriots are grown too shrewd to be sincere,
And we too wise to trust them.   He that takes
Deep in his soft credulity the stamp
Design'd by loud declaimers on the part
Of liberty, themselves the slaves of lust,
Incurs derision for his easy faith
And lack of knowledge, and with cause enough:
For when was public virtue to be found
Where private was not? Can he love the whole
Who loves no part? He be a nation's friend,
Who is, in truth, the friend of no man there?
Can he be strenuous in his country's cause
Who slights the charities, for whose dear sake
That country, if at all, must be belov'd?

　　'Tis therefore sober and good men are sad
For England's glory, seeing it wax pale
And sickly, while her champions wear their hearts
So loose to private duty, that no brain,
Healthful and undisturb'd by factious fumes,
Can dream them trusty to the gen'ral weal.
Such were they not of old, whose temper'd blades
Dispers'd the shackles of usurp'd control,
And hew'd them link from link; then Albion's sons
Were sons indeed; they felt a filial heart
Beat high within them at a mother's wrongs;
And shining each in his domestic sphere,

N

Shone brighter still, once call'd to public view.
'Tis therefore many, whose sequester'd lot
Forbids their interference, looking on,
Anticipate perforce some dire event :
And, seeing the old castle of the state,
That promis'd once more firmness, so assail'd,
That all its tempest-beaten turrets shake,
Stand motionless expectants of its fall.
All has its date below ; the fatal hour
Was register'd in heav'n ere time began.
We turn to dust, and all our mightiest works
Die too : the deep foundations that we lay,
Time ploughs them up, and not a trace remains.
We build with what we deem eternal rock ;
A distant age asks where the fabric stood ;
And in the dust, sifted and search'd in vain,
The undiscoverable secret sleeps.

But there is yet a liberty, unsung
By poets, and by senators unprais'd,
Which monarchs cannot grant, nor all the pow'rs
Of earth and hell confed'rate, take away :
A liberty, which persecution, fraud,
Oppression, prisons, have no pow'r to bind ;
Which, whoso tastes, can be enslav'd no more.
'Tis liberty of heart, deriv'd from heav'n ;
Bought with his blood who gave it to mankind,
And seal'd with the same token ! It is held -
By charter, and that charter sanction'd sure
By th' unimpeachable and awful oath
And promise of a God ! His other gifts
All bear the royal stamp that speaks them his,

And are august; but this transcends them all.
His other works, the visible display
Of all-creating energy and might,
Are grand, no doubt, and worthy of the word,
That, finding an interminable space
Unoccupied, has fill'd the void so well,
And made so sparkling what was dark before.
But these are not his glory.   Man, 'tis true,
Smit with the beauty of so fair a scene,
Might well suppose th' artificer divine
Meant it eternal, had he not himself
Pronounc'd it transient, glorious as it is,
And, still designing a more glorious far,
Doom'd it as insufficient for his praise.
These, therefore, are occasional, and pass;
Form'd for the confutation of the fool,
Whose lying heart disputes against a God;
That office serv'd, they must be swept away.
Not so the labors of his love: they shine
In other heav'ns than these that we behold,
And fade not.   There is a paradise that fears
No forfeiture, and of its fruits he sends
Large prelibation oft to saints below.
Of these the first in order, and the pledge
And confident assurance of the rest,
Is liberty :....a flight into his arms
Ere yet mortality's fine threads give way,
A clear escape from tyranizing lust,
And full immunity from penal woe.

  Chains are the portion of revolted man,
Stripes and a dungeon; and his body serves

The triple purpose. In that sickly, foul,
Opprobrious residence, he finds them all.
Propense his heart to idols, he is held
In silly dotage on created things,
Careless of their Creator. And that low
And sordid gravitation of his pow'rs
To a vile clod so draws him, with such force
Resistless from the centre he should seek,
That he at last forgets it. All his hopes
Tend downward; his ambition is to sink,
To reach a depth profounder still, and still
Profounder, in the fathomless abyss
Of folly, plunging in pursuit of death.
But, ere he gain the comfortless repose
He seeks, and acquiescence of his soul,
In heav'n-renouncing exile, he endures....
What does he not? from lusts oppos'd in vain,
And self-reproaching conscience. He foresees
The fatal issue to his health, fame, peace,
Fortune, and dignity; the loss of all
That can enoble man, and make frail life,
Short as it is, supportable. Still worse,
Far worse than all the plagues with which his sins
Infect his happiest moments, he forebodes
Ages of hopeless mis'ry. Future death,
And death still future. Not an hasty stroke,
Like that which sends him to the dusty grave;
But unrepealable enduring death!
Scripture is still a trumpet to his fears:
What none can prove a forg'ry, may be true;
What none but bad men wish exploded, must.
That scruple checks him. Riot is not loud,

Nor drunk enough to drown it.   In the midst
Of laughter his compunctions are sincere ;
And he abhors the jest by which he shines.
Remorse begets reform.   His master-lust
Falls first before his resolute rebuke,
And seems dethron'd and vanquish'd.   Peace ensues,
But spurious and short-liv'd ; the puny child
Of self-congratulating pride, begot
On fancied innocence.   Again he falls,
And fights again ; but finds his best essay
A presage ominous, portending still
Its own dishonor by a worse relapse.
Till nature, unavailing nature, foil'd
So oft, and wearied in the vain attempt,
Scoffs at her own performance.   Reason now
Takes part with appetite, and pleads the cause,
Perversely, which of late she so condemn'd ;
With shallow shifts and old devices, worn
And tatter'd in the service of debauch,
Cov'ring his shame from his offended sight.

"Hath God indeed giv'n appetites to man,
"And stor'd the earth so plenteously with means
"To gratify the hunger of his wish;
"And doth he reprobate, and will he damn,
"The use of his own bounty ? making first
"So frail a kind, and then enacting laws
"So strict, that less than perfect must despair ?
"Falsehood! which whoso but suspects of truth
"Dishonors God, and makes a slave of man.
"Do they themselves, who undertake for hire
"The teacher's office, and dispense at large
                        N 2

" Their weekly dole of edifying strains,
" Attend to their own music ? have they faith
" In what, with such solemnity of tone
" And gesture, they propound to our belief ?
" Nay...conduct hath the loudest tongue. The voice
" Is but an instrument, on which the priest
" May play what tune he pleases. In the deed,
" The unequivocal authentic deed,
" We find sound argument, we read the heart."

  Such reas'nings (if that name must need belong
T' excuses in which reason has no part)
Serve to compose a spirit well inclin'd
To live on terms of amity with vice,
And sin without disturbance. Often urg'd,
(As often as libidinous discourse
Exhausted, he resorts to solemn themes
Of theological and grave import)
They gain at last his unreserv'd assent ;
Till, harden'd his heart's temper in the forge
Of lust, and on the anvil of despair,
He slights the strokes of conscience. Nothing moves,
Or nothing much, his constancy in ill ;
Vain tamp'ring has but foster'd his disease ;
'Tis desp'rate, and he sleeps the sleep of death !
Haste now, philosopher, and set him free.
Charm the deaf serpeant wisely. Make him hear
Of rectitude and fitness, moral truth
How lovely, and the moral sense how sure,
Consulted and obey'd, to guide his steps
Directly to the FIRST AND ONLY FAIR.
Spare not in such a cause. Spend all the pow'rs

Of rant and rhapsody in virtue's praise:
Be most sublimely good, verbosely grand,
And with poetic trappings grace thy prose,
Till it out-mantle all the pride of verse....
Ah, tinkling cymbal, and high sounding brass,   ·
Smitten in vain! such music cannot charm
Th' eclipse that intercepts truth's heav'nly beam,
And chills and darkens a wide wand'ring soul.
The STILL SMALL VOICE is wanted. He must speak,
Whose word leaps forth at once to its effect;
Who calls for things that are not, and they come.

    Grace makes the slave a freeman. 'Tis a change
That turns to ridicule the turgid speech
And stately tone of moralists, who boast
As if, like him of fabulous renown,
They had indeed ability to smooth
The shag of savage nature, and were each
An Orpheus, and omnipotent in song:
But transformation of apostate man
From fool to wise, from earthly to divine,
Is work for Him that made him.   He alone,
And He by means in philosophic eyes
Trivial and worthy of disdain, achieves
The wonder; humanizing what is brute
In the lost kind, extracting from the lips
Of asps their venom, overpow'ring strength
By weakness, and hostility by love.

    Patriots have toil'd, and in their country's cause
Bled nobly; and their deeds, as they deserve,
Receive proud recompense. We give in charge

Their names to the sweet lyre. Th' historic muse,
Proud of the treasure, marches with it down
To latest times; and sculpture, in her turn,
Gives bond in stone and ever-during brass
To guard them, and t' immortalize her trust:
But fairer wreaths are due, though never paid,
To those, who, posted at the shrine of truth,
Have fall'n in her defence. A patriot's blood,
Well spent in such a strife, may earn indeed,
And for a time ensure, to his lov'd land
The sweets of liberty and equal laws;
But martyrs struggle for a brighter prize,
And win it with more pain. Their blood is shed'
In confirmation of the noblest claim....
Our claim to feed upon immortal truth,
To walk with God, to be divinely free,
To soar, and to anticipate the skies!
Yet few remember them. They liv'd unknown
Till persecution dragg'd them into fame,
And chas'd them up to heav'n. Their ashes flew...
No marble tells us whither. With their names
No bard embalms and sanctifies his song:
And history, so warm on meaner themes,
Is cold on this. She execrates indeed
The tyranny that doom'd them to the fire,
But gives the glorious suff'rers little praise,*

He is the freeman whom the truth makes free,.
And all are slaves beside. There's not a chain
That hellish foes, confed'rate for his harm,
Can wind around him, but he casts it off

* See Hume.   1

With as much ease as Sampson his green wyths.
He looks abroad into the varied field
Of nature, and, though poor perhaps compar'd
With those whose mansions glitter in his sight,
Calls the delightful scen'ry all his own.
His are the mountains, and the valleys his,
And the resplendent rivers. His t' enjoy
With a propriety that none can feel,
But who, with filial confidence inspir'd,
Can lift to heav'n an unpresumptuous eye,
And smiling say...." My Father made them all !"
Are they not his by a peculiar right,
And by an emphasis of int'rest his,
Whose eye they fill with tears of holy joy,
Whose heart with praise, and whose exalted mind
With worthy thoughts of that unwearied love
That plann'd, and built, and still upholds, a world
So cloth'd with beauty for rebellious man?
Yes....ye may fill your garners, ye that reap
The loaded soil, and ye may waste much good
In senseless riot; but ye will not find,
In feast or in the chase, in song or dance,
A liberty like his, who, unimpeach'd
Of usurpation, and to no man's wrong,
Appropriates nature as his Father's work,
And has a richer use of yours than you.
He is indeed a freeman. Free by birth
Of no mean city; plann'd or ere the hills
Were built, the fountains open'd, or the sea
With all his roaring multitude of waves.
His freedom is the same in ev'ry state;
And no condition of this changeful life,

So manifold in cares, whose ev'ry day
Brings its own evil with it, makes it less :
For he has wings, that neither sickness, pain,
Nor penury, can cripple or confine.
No nook so narrow but he spreads them there
With ease, and is at large. Th' oppressor holds
His body bound ; but knows not what a range
His spirit takes, unconscious of a chain ;
And that to bind him is a vain attempt
Whom God delights in, and in whom he dwells.

Acquaint thyself with God, if thou wouldst taste
His works. Admitted once to his embrace,
Thou shalt perceive that thou wast blind before :
Thine eye shall be instructed ; and thine heart,
Made pure, shall relish, with divine delight
Till then unfelt, what hands divine have wrought.
Brutes graze the mountain-top, with faces prone
And eyes intent upon the scanty herb
It yields them ; or, recumbent on its brow,
Ruminate heedless of the scene outspread
Beneath, beyond, and stretching far away
From inland regions to the distant main.
Man views it, and admires ; but rests content
With what he views. The landscape has his praise
But not its Author. Unconcern'd who form'd
The pardise he sees, he finds it such,
And such well pleas'd to find it, asks no more.
Not so the mind that has been touch'd from heav'n
And in the school of sacred wisdom taught
To read his wonders, in whose thought the world,
Fair as it is, existed ere it was.

for its own sake merely, but for his
h more who fashion'd it, he gives it praise;
ie that, from earth resulting, as it ought,
arth's acknowledg'd Sov'reign, finds at once
aly just proprietor in him.
soul that sees him, or receives sublim'd
faculties, or learns at least t' employ
e worthily the pow'rs she own'd before,
ems in all things, what, with stupid gaze
;norance, till then she overlook'd....
y of heav'nly light, gilding all forms
estrial in the vast and the minute;
unambiguous footsteps of the God
) gives its lustre to an insect's wing,
wheels his throne upon the rolling worlds.
h conversant with heav'n, she often holds
i those fair ministers of light to man,
fill the skies nightly with silent pomp,
it conference.   Inquires what strains were they
i which heav'n rang, when ev'ry star, in haste
ratulate the new created earth,
forth a voice, and all the sons of God
.ted for joy...." Tell me, ye shining hosts,
at navigate a sea that knows no storms,
aeath a vault unsullied with a cloud,
rom your elevation, whence ye view
itinctly scenes invisible to man,
d systems of whose birth no tidings yet
ve reach'd this nether world, ye spy a race
'or'd as ours; transgressors from the womb,
d hasting to a grave, yet doom'd to rise,
d to possess a brighter heav'n than yours?

" As one, who, long detain'd on foreign shores
" Pants to return, and when he sees afar
" His country's weather-bleach'd and batter'd rock
" From the green wave emerging, darts an eye
" Radiant with joy towards the happy land ;
" So I with animated hopes behold,
" And many an aching wish, your beamy fires,
" That show like beacons in the blue abyss,
" Ordain'd to guide th' embodied spirit home,
" From toilsome life to never-ending rest.
" Love kindles as I gaze.   I feel desires
" That give assurance of their own success,
" And that, infus'd from heav'n, must thither tend.

    So reads he nature whom the lamp of truth
Illuminates.   Thy lamp, mysterious word !
Which whoso sees no longer wanders lost,
With intellects bemaz'd in endless doubt,
But runs the road of wisdom.   Thou hast built,
With means that were not, till by thee employ'd,
Worlds that had never been, hadst thou in streng
Been less, or less benevolent than strong.
They are thy witnesses, who speak thy pow'r
And goodness infinite, but speak in ears
That hear not, or receive not their report.
In vain thy creatures testify of thee,
Till thou proclaim thyself.   Theirs is indeed
A teaching voice ; but 'tis the praise of thine,
That whom it teaches it makes prompt to learn,
And with the boon gives talents for its use.
Till thou art heard, imaginations vain
Possess the heart, and fables false as hell :

Yet, deem'd oracular, lure down to death
The uninform'd and heedless souls of men.
We give to chance, blind chance, ourselves as blind,
The glory of thy work; which yet appears
Perfect and unimpeachable of blame,
Challenging human scrutiny, and prov'd
Then skilful most when most severely judg'd.
But chance is not; or is not where thou reign'st:
Thy providence forbids that fickle pow'r
(If pow'r she be that works but to confound)
To mix her wild vagaries with thy laws.
Yet thus we dote, refusing while we can
Instruction, and inventing to ourselves
Gods, such as guilt makes welcome; gods that sleep,
Or disregard our follies, or that sit
Amus'd spectators of this bustling stage.
Thee we reject, unable to abide
Thy purity, till pure as thou art pure;
Made such by thee, we love thee for that cause
For which we shunn'd and hated thee before.
Then we are free. Then liberty, like day,
Breaks on the soul, and by a flash from heav'n
Fires all the faculties with glorious joy.
A voice is heard that mortal ears hear not
Till thou hast touch'd them; 'tis the voice of song....
A loud hosanna sent from all thy works;
Which he that hears it with a shout repeats,
And adds his rapture to the gen'ral praise.
In that blest moment, Nature, throwing wide
Her veil opaque, discloses with a smile
The Author of her beauties, who, retir'd
Behind his own creation, works unseen

o

By the impure, and hears his pow'r denied.
Thou art the source and centre of all minds,
Their only point of rest, eternal Word!
From thee departing, they are lost, and rove
At random, without honor, hope, or peace.
From thee is all that soothes the life of man,
His high endeavor, and his glad success,
His strength to suffer, and his will to serve.
But oh thou bounteous Giver of all good,
Thou art of all thy gifts, thyself the crown!
Give what thou canst, without thee we are poor;
And with thee rich, take what thou wilt away.

THE TASK,

A POEM.

BOOK VI.

ARGUMENT OF THE SIXTH BOOK.

Bells at a distance....Their effect....A fine noon in winter....A sheltered walk....Meditation better than books....Our familiarity with the course of nature makes it appear less wonderful than it is....The transformation that spring effects in a shrubbery described ....A mistake concerning the course of nature corrected....God maintains it by an unremitted act....The amusement fashionable at this hour of the day reproved....Animals happy, a delightful sight....Origin of cruelty to animals....That it is a great crime proved from scripture....That proof illustrated by a tale....A line drawn between the lawful and unlawful destruction of them.... Their good and useful properties insisted on....Apology for the encomiums bestowed by the author on animals....Instances of man's extravagant praise of man....The groans of the creation shall have an end....A view taken of the restoration of all things.... An invocation and an invitation of him who shall bring it to pass ....The retired man vindicated from the charge of uselessness.... Conclusion.

THE TASK.

BOOK VI.

THE WINTER WALK AT NOON.

THERE is in souls a sympathy with sounds;
And, as the mind is pitch'd, the ear is pleas'd
With melting airs, or martial, brisk, or grave:
Some chord in unison with what we hear
Is touch'd within us, and the heart replies.
How soft the music of those village bells,
Falling at intervals upon the ear
In cadence sweet, now dying all away,
Now pealing loud again, and louder still,
Clear and sonorous, as the gale comes on!
With easy force it opens all the cells
Where mem'ry slept. Wherever I have heard
A kindred melody, the scene recurs,
And with it all its pleasures and its pains.
Such comprehensive views the spirit takes,
That in a few short moments I retrace
(As in a map the voyager his course)
The windings of my way through many years.
Short as in retrospect the journey seems,
It seem'd not always short; the rugged path,
And prospect oft so dreary and forlorn,

Mov'd many a sigh at its disheart'ning length.
Yet, feeling present evils, while the past
Faintly impress the mind, or not at all,
How readily we wish time spent revok'd,
That we might try the ground again, where once
(Through inexperience, as we now perceive)
We miss'd that happiness we might have found!
Some friend is gone, perhaps his son's best friend!
A father, whose authority, in show
When most severe, and must'ring all its force,
Was but the graver countenance of love;
Whose favor, like the clouds of spring, might low'r,
And utter now and then an awful voice,
But had a blessing in its darkest frown,
Threat'ning at once, and nourishing the plant.
We lov'd, but not enough, the gentle hand
That rear'd us.   At a thoughtless age, allur'd
By ev'ry gilded folly, we renounc'd
His shelt'ring side, and wilfully forewent
That converse which we now in vain regret.
How gladly would the man recall to life
The boy's neglected sire! a mother too,
That softer friend, perhaps more gladly still,
Might he demand them at the gates of death.
Sorrow has, since they went, subdu'd and tam'd
The playful humor; he could now endure,
(Himself grown sober in the vale of tears)
And feel a parent's presence no restraint.
But not to understand a treasure's worth
Till time has stol'n away the slighted good,
Is cause of half the poverty we feel,
And makes the world the wilderness it is.

The few that pray at all pray oft amiss,
And, seeking grace t' improve the prize they hold,
Would urge a wiser suit than asking more.

The night was winter in his roughest mood;
The morning sharp and clear. But now at noon
Upon the southern side of the slant hills,
And where the woods fence-off the northern blast,
The season smiles, resigning all its rage,
And has the warmth of May. The vault is blue
Without a cloud, and white without a speck
The dazzling splendor of the scene below.
Again the harmony comes o'er the vale;
And through the trees I view th' embattled tow'r
Whence all the music. I again perceive
The soothing influence of the wafted strains,
And settle in soft musings as I tread
The walk, still verdant, under oaks and elms,
Whose outspread branches overarch the glade.
The roof, though moveable through all its length
As the wind sways it, has yet well suffic'd,
And, intercepting in their silent fall
The frequent flakes, has kept a path for me.
No noise is here, or none that hinders thought.
The red-breast warbles still, but is content
With slender notes, and more than half suppress'd:
Pleas'd with his solitude, and flitting light
From spray to spray, where'er he rests he shakes
From many a twig the pendent drops of ice,
That tinkle in the wither'd leaves below.
Stillness, accompanied with sounds so soft,
Charms more than silence. Meditation here

May think down hours to moments. Here the heart
May give an useful lesson to the head,
And learning wiser grow without his books.
Knowledge and wisdom, far from being one,
Have oft times no connexion. Knowledge dwells
In heads replete with thoughts of other men;
Wisdom in minds attentive to their own.
Knowledge, a rude unprofitable mass,
The mere materials with which wisdom builds,
Till smooth'd and squar'd and fitted to its place,
Does but encumber whom it seems t' enrich.
Knowledge is proud that he has learn'd so much;
Wisdom is humble that he knows no more.
Books are not seldom talismans and spells,
By which the magic arts of shrewder wits
Holds an unthinking multitude enthrall'd.
Some to the fascination of a name
Surrender judgment, hoodwink'd. Some the style
Infatuates, and through labyrinths and wilds
Of error, leads them by a tune entranc'd.
While sloth seduces more, too weak to bear
The insupportable fatigue of thought,
And swallowing, therefore, without pause or choice,
The total grist unsifted, husks and all.
But trees, and rivulets, whose rapid course
Defies the check of winter, haunts of deer,
And sheep-walks populous with bleating lambs,
And lanes in which the primrose ere her time
Peeps through the moss that clothes the hawthorn
    root,
Deceive no student. Wisdom there, and truth,
Not shy, as in the world, and to be won

By slow solicitation, seize at once
The roving thought, and fix it on themselves.

What prodigies can pow'r divine perform
More grand than it produces year by year,
And all in sight of inattentive man?
Familiar with th' effect we slight the cause,
And, in the constancy of nature's course,
The regular return of genial months,
And renovation of a faded world,
See nought to wonder at.   Should God again,
As once in Gibeon, interrupt the race
Of the undeviating and punctual sun,
How would the world admire! but speaks it less
An agency divine, to make him know
His moment when to sink and when to rise,
Age after age, than to arrest his course?
All we behold is miracle; but, seen
So duly, all is miracle in vain.
Where now the vital energy that mov'd
While summer was, the pure and subtile lymph
Through th' imperceptible meand'ring veins
Of leaf and flow'r? It sleeps; and th' icy touch
Of unprolific winter has impress'd
A cold stagnation on th' intestine tide.
But let the months go round, a few short months,
And all shall be restor'd. Those naked shoots,
Barren as lances, among which the wind
Makes wintry music, sighing as it goes,
Shall put their graceful foliage on again,
And, more aspiring, and with ample spread,
Shall boast new charms, and more than they have lost.

Then each in its peculiar honors clad,
Shall publish, even to the distant eye,
Its family and tribe.   Labernum, rich
In streaming gold; syringa, iv'ry pure;
The scentless and the scented rose; this red
And of a humble growth, the other* tall,
And throwing up into the darkest gloom
Of neighb'ring cypress, or more sable yew,
Her silver globes, light as the foamy surf
That the wind severs from the broken wave;
The lilac, various in array, now white,
Now sanguine, and her beauteous head now set
With purple spikes pyramidal, as if,
Studious of ornament, yet unresolv'd
Which hue she most approv'd, she chose them all;
Copious of flow'rs the woodbine, pale and wan,
But well compensating her sickly looks
With never-cloying odors, early and late;
Hypericum, all bloom, so thick a swarm
Of flow'rs, like flies clothing her slender rods,
That scarce a leaf appears; mezerion, too,
Though leafless, well attir'd, and thick beset
With blushing wreaths, investing ev'ry spray;
Althæa with the purple eye; the broom,
Yellow and bright, as bullion unalloy'd,
Her blossoms; and luxuriant above all,
The jasmine, throwing wide her elegant sweets,
The deep dark green of whose unvarnish'd leaf
Makes more conspicuous, and illumines more
The bright profusion of her scatter'd stars....
These have been, and these shall be in their day;

* The Gueldar-rose.

And all this uniform, uncolor'd scene,
Shall be dismantled of its fleecy load,
And flush into variety again.
From dearth to plenty, and from death to life,
Is Nature's progress, when she lectures man
In heav'nly truth; evincing, as she makes
The grand transition, that there lives and works
A soul in all things, and that soul is God.
The beauties of the wilderness are his,
That make so gay the solitary place
Where no eye sees them.   And the fairer forms
That cultivation glories in, are his.
He sets the bright procession on its way,
And marshals all the order of the year;
He marks the bounds which winter may not pass,
And blunts his pointed fury; in its case,
Russet and rude, folds up the tender germ,
Uninjur'd, with inimitable art;
And, ere one flow'ry season fades and dies,
Designs the blooming wonders of the next.

Some say, that, in the origin of things,
When all creation started into birth,
The infant elements receiv'd a law,
From which they swerve not since. That under force
Of that controling ordinance they move,
And need not his immediate hand, who first
Prescrib'd their course, to regulate it now.
Thus dream they, and contrive to save a God
Th' incumbrance of his own concerns, and spare
The great artificer of all that moves
The stress of a continual act, the pain

Of unremitted vigilance and care,
As too laborious and severe a task.
So man, the moth, is not afraid, it seems,
To span omnipotence, and measure might,
That knows no measure, by the scanty rule
And standard of his own, that is to-day,
And is not ere to-morrow's sun go down!
But how should matter occupy a charge,
Dull as it is, and satisfy a law
So vast in its demands, unless impell'd
To ceaseless service by a ceaseless force,
And under pressure of some conscious cause?
The Lord of all, himself through all diffus'd,
Sustains, and is the life of all that lives.
Nature is but a name for an effect,
Whose cause is God.   He feeds the secret fire
By which the mighty process is maintain'd,
Who sleeps not, is not weary; in whose sight
Slow-circling ages are as transient days;
Whose work is without labor; whose designs
No flaw deforms, no difficulty thwarts;
And whose beneficence no charge exhausts.
Him blind antiquity profan'd, not serv'd,
With self-taught rites, and under various names,
Female and male, Pomona, Pales, Pan,
And Flora, and Vertumnus; peopling earth
With tutelary goddesses and gods
That were not; and commanding, as they would,
To each some province, garden, field, or grove.
But all are under one.   One spirit....He
Who wore the platted thorns with bleeding brows
Rules universal nature.   Not a flow'r

But shows some touch, in freckle, streak, or stain,
Of his unrivall'd pencil.   He inspires
Their balmy odors, and imparts their hues,
And bathes their eyes with nectar, and includes,
In grains as countless as the sea-side sands,
The forms with which he sprinkles all the earth.
Happy who walks with him! whom what he finds
Of flavor or of scent in fruit or flow'r,
Or what he views of beautiful or grand
In nature, from the broad majestic oak
To the green blade that twinkles in the sun,
Prompts with remembrance of a present God!
His presence, who made all so fair, perceiv'd,
Makes all still fairer.   As with him no scene
Is dreary, so with him all seasons please.
Though winter had been none, had man been true,
And earth be punish'd for its tenant's sake,
Yet not in vengeance; as this smiling sky,
So soon succeeding such an angry night,
And these dissolving snows, and this clear stream
Recov'ring fast its liquid music, prove.

    Who then, that has a mind well strung and tun'd
To contemplation, and within his reach
A scene so friendly to his fav'rite task,
Would waste attention at the chequer'd board,
His host of wooden warriors to and fro
Marching and counter-marching, with an eye
As fix'd as marble, with a forehead ridg'd
And furrow'd into storms, and with a hand
Trembling, as if eternity were hung
In balance on his conduct of a pin?....

P

Nor envies he aught more their idle sport,
Who pant with application misapplied
To trivial toys, and, pushing iv'ry balls
Across a velvet level, feel a joy
Akin to rapture when the bauble finds
Its destin'd goal, of difficult access....
Nor deems he wiser him, who gives his noon
To miss, the mercer's plague, from shop to shop
Wand'ring, and litt'ring with unfolded silks
The polish'd counter, and approving none,
Or promising with smiles to call again....
Nor him, who by his vanity seduc'd,
And sooth'd into a dream that he discerns
The diff'rence of a Guido from a daub,
Frequents the crowded auction: station'd there
As duly as the Langford of the show,
With glass at eye, and catalogue in hand,
And tongue accomplish'd in the fulsome cant
And pedantry that coxcombs learn with ease;
Oft as the price-deciding hammar falls
He notes it in his book, then raps his box,
Swears 'tis a bargain, rails at his hard fate
That he has let it pass....but never bids !

　Here, unmolested, through whatever sign
The sun proceeds, I wander. Neither mist,
Nor freezing sky nor sultry, checking me,
Nor stranger intermeddling with my joy.
Ev'n in the spring and play-time of the year,
That calls th' unwonted villager abroad
With all her little ones, a sportive train,
To gather king-cups in the yellow mead,

And prink their hair with daisies, or to pick
A cheap but wholesome sallad from the brook,
These shades are all my own.   The tim'rous hare,
Grown so familiar with her frequent guest,
Scarce shuns me ; and the stock-dove, unalarm'd,
Sits cooing in the pine-tree, nor suspends
His long love-ditty for my near approach.
Drawn from his refuge in some lonely elm
That age or injury has hallow'd deep,
Where, on his bed of wool and matted leaves,
He has outslept the winter, ventures forth
To frisk awhile, and bask in the warm sun,
The squirrel, flippant, pert, and full of play ;
He sees me, and at once, swift as a bird,
Ascends the neighb'ring beach ; there whisks his
        brush,
And perks his ears, and stamps and cries aloud,
With all the prettiness of feign'd alarm,
And anger insignificantly fierce.

    The heart is hard in nature, and unfit
For human fellowship, as being void
Of sympathy, and therefore dead alike
To love and friendship both, that is not pleas'd
With sight of animals enjoying life,
Nor feels their happiness augment his own.
The bounding fawn, that darts across the glade
When none pursues, through mere delight of heart,
And spirits buoyant with excess of glee ;
The horse as wanton, and almost as fleet,
That skims the spacious meadow at full speed,
Then stops and snorts, and, throwing high his heels,

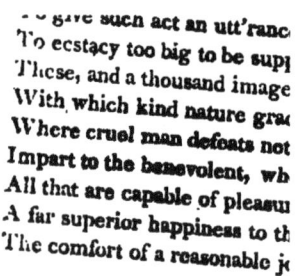

... give such act an utt'ranc
To ecstacy too big to be sup
These, and a thousand image
With which kind nature gra
Where cruel man defeats not
Impart to the benevolent, wh
All that are capable of pleasu
A far superior happiness to th
The comfort of a reasonable j

Man scarce had ris'n, obedi
Who form'd him from the dus
When he was crown'd as neve
God set the diadem upon his h
And angel choirs attended. W
The new made monarch, while
All happy, and all perfect in the
The creatures summon'd from
To see their sov'raign, and

So Eden was a scene of harmless sport,
Where kindness on his part who rul'd the whole
Begat a tranquil confidence in all,
And fear as yet was not, nor cause for fear.
But sin marr'd all; and the revolt of man,
That source of evils not exhausted yet,
Was punish'd with revolt of his from him.
Garden of God, how terrible the change
Thy groves and lawns then witness'd! Ev'ry heart,
Each animal of ev'ry name, conceiv'd
A jealousy and an instinctive fear,
And, conscious of some danger, either fled
Precipitate the loath'd abode of man,
Or growl'd defiance in such angry sort,
As taught him, too, to tremble in his turn.
Thus harmony and family accord
Were driv'n from Paradise; and in that hour
The seeds of cruelty, that since have swell'd
To such gigantic and enormous growth,
Were sown in human nature's fruitful soil.
Hence date the persecution and the pain
That man inflicts on all inferior kinds,
Regardless of their plaints. To make him sport,
To gratify the frenzy of his wrath,
Or his base gluttony, are causes good
And just, in his account, why bird and beast
Should suffer torture, and the streams be dyed
With blood of their inhabitants impal'd.
Earth groans beneath the burden of a war
Wag'd with defenceless innocence, while he,
Not satisfied to prey on all around,
Adds tenfold bitterness to death by pangs

Needless, and first torments ere he devours.
Now happiest they that occupy the scenes
The most remote from his abhor'd resort,
Whom once, as delegate of God on earth,
They fear'd, and as his perfect image, lov'd.
The wilderness is theirs, with all its caves,
Its hollow glens, its thickets, and its plains,
Unvisited by man.   There they are free,
And howl and roar as likes them, uncontrol'd;
Nor ask his leave to slumber or to play.
Woe to the tyrant, if he dare intrude
Within the confines of their wild domain!
The lion tells him....I am monarch here!
And, if he spare him, spares him on the terms
Of royal mercy, and through gen'rous scorn
To read a victim trembling at his foot.
In measure, as by force of instinct drawn,
Or by necessity constrain'd, they live
Dependent upon man; those in his fields,
These at his crib, and some beneath his roof.
They prove too often at how dear a rate
He sells protection....Witness at his foot
The spaniel dying, for some venial fault,
Under dissection of the knotted scourge....
Witness the patient ox, with stripes and yells
Driv'n to the slaughter, goaded, as he runs,
To madness; while the savage at his heels
Laughs at the frantic suff'rer's fury, spent
Upon the guiltless passenger o'erthrown.
He too, is witness, noblest of the train
That wait on man, the flight-performing horse:
With unsuspecting readiness he takes

His murd'rer on his back, and, push'd all day,
With bleeding sides and flanks that heave for life,
To the far-distant goal, arrives and dies.
So little mercy shows who needs so much!
Does law, so jealous in the cause of man,
Denounce no doom on the delinquent?....None.
He lives, and o'er his brimming beaker boasts
(As if barbarity were high desert)
Th' inglorious feat, and, clamorous in praise
Of the poor brute, seems wisely to suppose
The honors of his matchless horse his own!
But many a crime, deem'd innocent on earth,
Is register'd in heav'n; and these, no doubt,
Have each their record, with a curse annex'd.
Man may dismiss compassion from his heart,
But God will never.   When he charg'd the Jew
T' assist his foe's down-fallen beast to rise;
And when the bush-exploring boy, that seiz'd
The young, to let the parent bird go free;
Prov'd he not plainly that his meaner works
Are yet his care, and have an int'rest all,
All, in the universal Father's love?
On Noah, and in him on all mankind,
The charter was conferr'd, by which we hold
The flesh of animals in fee, and claim
O'er all we feed on pow'r of life and death.
But read the instrument, and mark it well;
Th' oppression of a tyrannous control
Can find no warrant there.   Feed, then, and yield
Thanks for thy food.   Carnivorous, through sin,
Feed on the slain, but spare the living brute!

The Governor of all, himself to all
So bountiful, in whose attentive ear
The unfledg'd raven and the lion's whelp
Plead not in vain for pity on the pangs
Of hunger unassuag'd, has interpos'd,
Not seldom, his avenging arm, to smite
Th' injurious trampler upon nature's law,
That claims forbearance even for a brute.
He hates the hardness of a Balaam's heart;
And, prophet as he was, he might not strike
The blameless animal without rebuke,
On which he rode.   Her opportune offence
Sav'd him, or th' unrelenting seer had died.
He sees that human equity is slack
To interfere, though in so just a cause;
And makes the task his own.   Inspiring dumb
And helpless victims with a sense so keen
Of inj'ry, with such knowledge of their strength,
And such sagacity to take revenge,
That oft the beast has seem'd to judge the man.
An ancient, not a legendary tale,
By one of sound intelligence rehears'd,
(If such who plead for Providence may seem
In modern eyes) shall make the doctrine clear....

Where England, stretch'd towards the setting sun,
Narrow and long, o'erlooks the western wave,
Dwelt young Misagathus; a scorner he
Of God and goodness, atheist in ostent;
Vicious in act, in temper savage-fierce.
He journey'd; and his chance was as he went,
To join a trav'ller, of far diff'rent note....

Evander, fam'd for piety, for years
Deserving honor, but for wisdom more.
Fame had not left the venerable man
A stranger to the manners of the youth,
Whose face, too, was familiar to his view.
Their way was on the margin of the land,
O'er the green summit of the rocks, whose base
Beats back the roaring surge, scarce heard so high.
The charity that warm'd his heart was mov'd
At sight of the man-monster.   With a smile
Gentle, and affable, and full of grace,
As fearful of offending whom he wish'd
Much to persuade, he plied his ear with truths
Not harshly thunder'd forth or rudely press'd,
But, like his purpose, gracious, kind, and sweet.
" And dost thou dream," th' impenetrable man
Exclaim'd, " that me the lullabies of age,
" And fantasies of dotards, such as thou,
" Can cheat, or move a moment's fear in me ?
" Mark now the proof I give thee, that the brave
" Need no such aids as superstition lends
" To steel their hearts against the dread of death."
He spoke, and to the precipice at hand
Push'd with a madman's fury.   Fancy shrinks,
And the blood thrills and curdles, at the thought
Of such a gulph as he design'd his grave.
But, though the felon on his back could dare
The dreadful leap, more rational, his steed
Declin'd the death, and, wheeling swiftly round,
Or e'er his hoof had press'd the crumbling verge,
Baffled his rider, sav'd against his will !
The frenzy of the brain may be redress'd .

By med'cine well applied, but without grace
The heart's insanity admits no cure.
Enrag'd the more, by what might have reform'd
His horrible intent, again he sought
Destruction, with a zeal to be destroy'd,
With sounding whip, and rowels dyed in blood.
But still in vain. The Providence that meant
A longer date to the far nobler beast,
Spar'd yet again th' ignobler, for his sake.
And now, his prowess prov'd, and his sincere
Incurable obduracy evinc'd,
His rage grew cool; and, pleas'd perhaps t' have
          earn'd
So cheaply the renown of that attempt,
With looks of some complacence he resum'd
His road, deriding much the blank amaze
Of good Evander, still where he was left
Fix'd motionless, and petrified with dread.
So on they far'd. Discourse on other themes
Ensuing, seem'd t' obliterate the past;
And, tamer far for so much fury shown,
(As is the course of rash and fiery men)
The rude companion smil'd, as if transform'd.
But 'twas a transient calm. A storm was near,
An unsuspected storm. His hour was come.
The impious challenger of pow'r divine
Was now to learn, that Heav'n, though slow to wrath,
Is never with impunity defied.
His horse, as he had caught his master's mood,
Snorting, and starting into sudden rage,
Unbidden, and not now to be control'd,
Rush'd to the cliff, and, having reach'd it, stood:

At once the shock unseated him: he flew
Sheer o'er the craggy barrier; and, immers'd
Deep in the flood, found, when he sought it not,
The death he had deserv'd....and died alone !
So God wrought double justice; made the fool
The victim of his own tremendous choice,
And taught a brute the way to safe revenge.

  I would not enter on my list of friends
(Though grac'd with polish'd manners and fine sense,
Yet wanting sensibility) the man
Who needlessly sets foot upon a worm.
An inadvertent step may crush the snail
That crawls at ev'ning in the public path ;
But he that has humanity, forewarn'd,
Will tread aside, and let the reptile live.
The creeping vermin, loathsome to the sight,
And charg'd perhaps with venom, that intrudes,
A visitor unwelcome, into scenes
Sacred to neatness and repose....th' alcove,
The chamber, or refectory....may die :
A necessary act incurs no blame.
Not so when held within their proper bounds,
And guiltless of offence, they range the air,
Or take their pastime in the spacious field :
There they are priviledg'd ; and he that hunts
Or harms them there is guilty of a wrong,
Disturbs th' economy of nature's realm,
Who, when she form'd, design'd them an abode.
The sum is this....If man's convenience, health,
Or safety, interfere, his rights and claims
Are paramount, and must extinguish theirs.

'ı Else they are all....the meanest things that are....
As free to live, and to enjoy that life,
As God was free to form them at the first,
Who, in his sov'reign wisdom, made them all.
Ye, therefore, who love mercy, teach your sons
To love it too. The spring-time of our years
Is soon dishonor'd and defil'd in most
By budding ills, that ask a prudent hand
To check them. But, alas! none sooner shoots,
If unrestrain'd, into luxuriant growth,
Than cruelty, most dev'lish of them all.
Mercy to him that shows it, is the rule
And righteous limitation of its act,
By which Heav'n moves in pard'ning guilty man;
And he that shows none, being ripe in years,
And conscious of the outrage he commits,
Shall seek it, and not find it, in his turn.

  Distinguish'd much by reason, and still more
By our capacity of grace divine,
From creatures that exist but for our sake,
Which, having serv'd us, perish, we are held
Accountable; and God, some future day,
Will reckon with us roundly for th' abuse
Of what he deems no mean or trivial trust.
Superior as we are, they yet depend
Not more on human help than we on theirs.
Their strength, or speed, or vigilance, were giv'n
In aid of our defects. In some are found
Such teachable and apprehensive parts,
That man's attainments in his own concerns,
Match'd with th' expertness of the brute's in theirs,

Are oft times vanquish'd and thrown far behind.
Some show that nice sagacity of smell,
And read with such discernment, in the port
And figure of the man, his secret aim,
That oft we owe our safety to a skill
We could not teach, and must despair to learn.
But learn we might, if not too proud to stoop
To quadruped instructors, many a good
And useful quality, and virtue too,
Rarely exemplified among ourselves.
Attachment never to be wean'd, or chang'd,
By any change of fortune ; proof alike
Against unkindness, absence, and neglect;
Fidelity, that neither bribe nor threat
Can move or warp ; and gratitude for small
And trivial favors, lasting as the life,
And glist'ning even in the dying eye.

   Man praises man.   Desert in arts or arms
Wins public honor; and ten thousand sit
Patiently present at a sacred song,
Commemoration-mad; content to hear
(Oh wonderful effect of music's pow'r !)
Messiah's eulogy for Handel's sake !
But less, methinks, than sacrilege might serve....
(For, was it less ? what heathen would have dar'd
To strip Jove's statue of his oaken wreath,
And hang it up in honor of a man !)
Much less might serve, when all that we design
Is but to gratify an itching ear,
And give the day to a musician's praise.
Remember Handel ? Who, that was not born
Deaf as the dead to harmony, forgets,   ·

Q

Or can, the more than Homer of his age ?
Yes....we remember him; and, while we praise
A talent so divine, remember too,
That his most holy book from whom it came,
Was never meant, was never us'd before,
To buckram out the mem'ry of a man.
But hush!....the muse perhaps is too severe ;
And, with a gravity beyond the size
And measure of th' offence, rebukes a deed
Less impious than absurd, and owing more
To want of judgment than to wrong design.
So in the chapel of old Ely House,
When wand'ring Charles, who meant to be the third,
Had fled from William, and the news was fresh,
The simple clerk, but loyal, did announce,
And eke did rear right merrily, two staves,
Sung to the praise and glory of King George !
Man praises man ; and Garrick's mem'ry next,
When time hath somewhat mellow'd it, and made
The idol of our worship while he liv'd
The god of our idolatry once more,
Shall have its altar ; and the world shall go
In pilgrimage to bow before his shrine.
The theatre, too small, shall suffocate
Its squeez'd contents, and more than it admits
Shall sigh at their exclusion, and return
Ungratified.   For there some noble lord
Shall stuff his shoulders with King Richard's bunch,
Or wrap himself in Hamlet's inky cloak,
And strut, and storm, and straddle, stamp, and stare,
To show the world how Garrick did not act....
For Garrick was a worshipper himself;
He drew the liturgy, and fram'd the rites

And solemn ceremonial of the day,
And call'd the world to worship on the banks
Of Avon, fam'd in song.   Ah, pleasant proof
That piety has still in human hearts
Some place, a spark or two not yet extinct.
The mulb'ry-tree was hung with blooming wreaths;
The mulb'ry-tree stood centre of the dance;
The mulb'ry-tree was hymn'd with dulcet airs;
And from his touch-wood trunk the mulb'ry-tree
Supplied such relics as devotion holds
Still sacred, and preserves with pious care.
So 'twas an hallow'd time: decorum reign'd,
And mirth without offence.   No few return'd,
Doubtless, much edified, and all refresh'd.
....Man praises man.   The rabble, all alive,
From tippling-benches, cellars, stalls, and styes,
Swarm in the streets.   The statesman of the day,
A pompous and slow-moving pageant comes.
Some shout him, and some hang upon his car,
To gaze in 's eyes, and bless him.   Maidens wave
Their 'kerchiefs, and old women weep for joy:
While others, not so satisfied, unhorse
The gilded equipage, and, turning loose
His steeds, usurp a place they well deserve.
Why? what has charm'd them?   Hath he sav'd the
          state?
No.   Doth he purpose its salvation?   No.
Enchanting novelty, that moon at full,
That finds out ev'ry crevice of the head
That is not sound and perfect, hath in theirs
Wrought this disturbance.   But the wane is near,
And his own cattle must suffice him soon.
Thus idly do we waste the breath of praise,

And dedicate a tribute, in its use
And just direction sacred, to a thing
Doom'd to the dust, or lodg'd already there !
Encomium in old time was poet's work ;
But poets having lavishly long since
Exhausted all materials of the art,
The task now falls into the public hand ;
And I, contented with an humble theme,
Have pour'd my stream of panegyric down
The vale of nature, where it creeps, and winds.
Among her lovely works with a secure
And unambitious course, reflecting clear,
If not the virtues, yet the worth, of brutes.
And I am recompens'd, and deem the toils
Of poetry not lost, if verse of mine
May stand between an animal and woe,
And teach one tyrant pity for his drudge.

The groans of nature in this nether world,
Which Heav'n has heard for ages, have an end.
Foretold by prophets, and by poets sung,
Whose fire was kindled at the prophet's lamp,
The time of rest, the promis'd sabbath, comes.
Six thousand years of sorrow have well nigh
Fulfill'd their tardy and disastrous course
Over a sinful world ; and what remains
Of this tempestuous state of human things,
Is merely as the working of a sea
Before a calm, that rocks itself to rest :
For HE, whose car the winds are, and the clouds
The dust that waits upon the sultry march,
When sin hath mov'd him, and his wrath is hot,

Shall visit earth in mercy ; shall descend,
Propitious, in his chariot pav'd with love ;
And what his storms have blasted and defac'd
For man's revolt, shall with a smile repair.

   Sweet is the harp of prophecy ; too sweet
Not to be wrong'd by a mere mortal touch :
Nor can the wonders it records be sung
To meaner music, and not suffer loss.
But, when a poet, or when one like me,
Happy to rove among poetic flow'rs,
Though poor in skill to rear them, lights at last
On some fair theme, some theme divinely fair,
Such is the impulse and the spur he feels
To give it praise proportion'd to its worth,
That not t' attempt it, arduous as he deems
The labor, were a task more arduous still.

   Oh scenes surpassing fable, and yet true,
Scenes of accomplish'd bliss ! which who can see,
Though but in distant prospect, and not feel
His soul refresh'd with foretaste of the joy ?
Rivers of gladness water all the earth,
And clothe all climes with beauty ; the reproach
Of barrenness is past. The fruitful field
Laughs with abundance ; and the land, once lean,
Or fertile only in its own disgrace,
Exults to see its thistly curse repeal'd.
The various seasons woven into one,
And that one season an eternal spring,
The garden fears no blight, and needs no fence,
For there is none to covet, all are full.

The lion, and the libbard, and the bear
Graze with the fearless flocks; all bask at noon
Together, or all gambol in the shade
Of the same grove, and drink one common stream.
Antipathies are none.   No foe to man
Lurks in the serpent now: the mother sees,
And smiles to see, her infant's playful hand
Stretch'd forth to dally with the crested worm,
To stroke his azure neck, or to receive
The lambent homage of his arrowy tongue.
All creatures worship man, and all mankind
One Lord, one Father.   Error has no place:
That creeping pestilence is driv'n away;
The breath of heav'n has chas'd it.   In the heart
No passion touches a discordant string,
But all his harmony and love.   Disease
Is not: the pure and uncontam'nate blood
Holds its due course, nor fears the frost of age.
One song employs all nations; and all cry,
" Worthy the Lamb, for he was slain for us !"
The dwellers in the vales and on the rocks
Shout to each other, and the mountain tops
From distant mountains catch the flying joy;
Till, nation after nation taught the strain,
Earth rolls the rapturous hosannas round.
Behold the measure of the promise fill'd;
See Salem built, the labor of a God!
Bright as a sun the sacred city shines;
All kingdoms and all princes of the earth
Flock to that light; the glory of all lands
Flows into her; unbounded is her joy,
And endless her increase.   Thy rams are there,

*Nebaioth, and the flocks of Kedar there;
The looms of Ormus, and the mines of Ind,
And Saba's spicy groves, pay tribute there.
Praise is in all her gates: upon her walls,
And in her streets, and in her spacious courts,.
Is heard salvation.   Eastern Java there
Kneels with the native of the farthest west;
And Ethiopia spreads abroad the hand,
And worships.   Her report has travell'd forth
Into all lands.   From ev'ry clime they come
To see thy beauty and to share thy joy,
O Sion! an assembly such as earth
Saw never, such as heav'n stoops down to see..

 Thus heav'n-ward all things tend.   For all were
  once
Perfect, and all must be at length restor'd.
So God has greatly purpos'd; who would else
In his dishonor'd works himself endure
Dishonor, and be wrong'd without redress.
Haste, then, and wheel away a shatter'd world,
Ye slow-revolving seasons! we would see
(A sight to which our eyes are strangers yet)
A world that does not dread and hate his laws,
And suffer for its crime; would learn how fair
The creature is that God pronounces good,.
How pleasant in itself what pleases him.
Here ev'ry drop of honey hides a sting;
Worms wind themselves into our sweetest flow'rs;
And ev'n the joy that haply some poor heart

 * Nebaioth and Kedar, the sons of Ishmael; and progenitors of
the Arabs, in the prophetic scripture here alluded to, may be rea-
sonably considered as representatives of the Gentiles at large.

Derives from heav'n, pure as the fountain is,
Is sullied in the stream, taking a taint
From touch of human lips, at best impure.
Oh for a world in principle as chaste
As this is gross and selfish! over which
Custom and prejudice shall bear no sway,
That govern all things here, should'ring aside
The meek and modest truth, and forcing her
To seek a refuge from the tongue of strife
In nooks obscure, far from the ways of men :....
Where violence shall never lift the sword,
Nor cunning justify the proud man's wrong,
Leaving the poor no remedy but tears :....
Where he that fills an office shall esteem
Th' occasion it presents of doing good
More than the perquisite :....where law shall speak
Seldom, and never but as wisdom prompts
And equity; not jealous more to guard
A worthless form, than to decide aright :....
Where fashion shall not sanctify abuse,
Nor smooth good breeding (supplemental grace)
With lean performance ape the work of love !

    Come then, and, added to thy many crowns,
Receive yet one, the crown of all the earth,
Thou who alone art worthy ! It was thine
By ancient cov'nant, ere nature's birth ;
And thou hast made it thine by purchase since,
And overpaid its value with thy blood.
Thy saints proclaim thee king ; and in their hearts
Thy title is engraven with a pen
Dipp'd in the fountain of eternal love.
Thy saints proclaim thee king ; and thy delay

:ourage to their foes, who, could they see
wn of thy last advent, long desir'd,
 creep into the bowels of the hills,
:e for safety to the falling rocks.
ry spirit of the world is tir'd
ıwn taunting question, ask'd so long,
re is the promise of your Lord's approach?"
fidel has shot his bolts away,
.s exhausted quiver yielding none,
ans the blunted shafts that have recoil'd,
ms them at the shield of truth again.
:il is rent, rent too by priestly hands,
ides divinity from mortal eyes;
l the mysteries to faith propos'd,
d and traduc'd, are cast aside,
less, to the moles and to the bats.
ıow are deem'd the faithful, and are prais'd,
:onstant only in rejecting thee,
hy Godhead with a martyr's zeal,
ıit their office for their error's sake.
and in love with darkness! yet ev'n these
y, compar'd with sycophants, who kneel
ıme adoring, and then preach thee man!
s thy church.   But how thy church may fare
ırld takes little thought. Who will may preach,
hat they will.   All pastors are alike
ıd'ring sheep, resolv'd to follow none.
ods divide them all....Pleasure and Gain.
:se they live, they sacrifice to these,
. their service wage perpetual war
onscience and with thee. Lust in their hearts,
ischief in their heads, they roam the earth
y upon each other; stubborn, fierce,

High-minded, foaming out their own disgrace. •
Thy prophets speak of such ; and, noting down
The features of the last degen'rate times,
Exhibit ev'ry lineament of these.
Come then, and, added to thy many crowns,
Receive yet one, as radiant as the rest,
Due to thy last and most effectual work,
Thy word fulfill'd, the conquest of a world!

  He is a happy man, whose life ev'n now
Shows somewhat of that happier life to come ;
Who, doom'd to an obscure but tranquil state,
Is pleas'd with it, and, were he free to choose,
Would make his fate his choice ; whom peace, the
          fruit
Of virtue, and whom virtue, fruit of faith,
Prepare for happiness ; bespeak him one ·
Content indeed to sojourn while he must
Below the skies, but having there his home.
The world o'erlooks him in her busy search
Of objects, more illustrious in her view ;
And, occupied as earnestly as she,   ·
Though more sublimely, he o'erlooks the world.
She scorns his pleasures, for she knows them not ;
He seeks not hers, for he has prov'd them vain.
He cannot skim the ground like summer birds   :
Pursuing gilded flies ; and such he deems   ··
Her honors, her emoluments, her joys.
Therefore in contemplation is his bliss,   · :
Whose pow'r is such, that whom she lifts from earth
She makes familiar with a heav'n unseen,   ·
And shows him glories yet to be reveal'd.
Not slothful he, though seeming unemploy'd,

And censur'd oft as useless. Stillest streams
Oft water fairest meadows, and the bird
That flutters least is longest on the wing.
Ask him, indeed, what trophies he has rais'd,
Or what achievements of immortal fame
He purposes, and he shall answer....None.
His warfare is within.   There unfatigu'd
His fervent spirit labors.   There he fights,
And there obtains fresh triumphs o'er himself,
And never with'ring wreaths, compar'd with which
The laurels that a Cæsar reaps are weeds.
Perhaps the self-approving haughty world,
That as she weeps him with her whistling silks
Scarce deigns to notice him, or, if she see,
Deems him a cypher in the works of God,
Receives advantage from his noiseless hours,
Of which she little dreams.   Perhaps she owes
Her sunshine and her rain, her blooming spring
And plenteous harvest, to the pray'r he makes,
When, Isaac like, the solitary saint
Walks forth to meditate at even-tide,
And think on her, who thinks not for herself.
Forgive him, then, thou bustler in concerns
Of little worth, an idler in the best,
If, author of no mischief and some good,
He seek his proper happiness by means
That may advance, but cannot hinder, thine.
Nor, though he tread the secret path of life,
Engage no notice, and enjoy much ease,
Account him an incumbrance on the state,
Receiving benefits, and rend'ring none.
His sphere though humble, if that humble sphere
Shine with his fair example, and though small

His influence, if that influence all be spent
In soothing sorrow and in quenching strife,
In aiding helpless indigence, in works
From which at least a grateful few derive
Some taste of comfort in a world of woe,
Then let the supercilious great confess
He serves his country, recompenses well
The state, beneath the shadow of whose vine
He sits secure, and in the scale of life
Holds no ignoble, though a slighted, place.
The man, whose virtues are more felt than seen,
Must drop indeed the hope of public praise;
But he may boast what few that win it can....
That, if his country stand not by his skill,
At least his follies have not wrought her fall.
Polite refinement offers him in vain
Her golden tube, through which a sensual world
Draws gross impurity, and likes it well,
The neat conveyance hiding all th' offence.
Not that he peevishly rejects a mode
Because that world adopts it.   If it bear
The stamp and clear impression of good sense,
And be not costly more than of true worth,
He puts it on, and for decorum sake,
Can wear it e'en as gracefully as she.
She judges of refinement by the eye,
He by the test of conscience, and a heart
Not soon deceiv'd; aware that what is base
No polish can make sterling; and that vice,
Though well perfum'd and elegantly dress'd,
Like an unburied carcase trick'd with flow'rs,
Is but a garnish'd nuisance, fitter far
For cleanly riddance than for fair attire.

So life glides smoothly and by stealth away,
More golden than that age of fabled gold
Renown'd in ancient song; not vex'd with care
Or stain'd with guilt, beneficent, approv'd
Of God and man, and peaceful in its end.
So glide my life away! and so at last,
My share of duties decently fulfill'd,
May some disease, not tardy to perform
Its destin'd office, yet with gentle stroke,
Dismiss me, weary, to a safe retreat
Beneath that turf that I have often trod.
It shall not grieve me, then, that once, when call'd
To dress a Sofa with the flow'rs of verse,
I play'd awhile, obedient to the fair,
With that light task; but soon, to please her more,
Whom flow'rs alone I knew would little please,
Let fall th' unfinish'd wreath, and rov'd for fruit;
Rov'd far, and gather'd much: some harsh, 'tis true,
Pick'd from the thorns and briers of reproof,
But wholesome, well digested; grateful some
To palates that can taste immortal truth;
Insipid else, and sure to be despis'd.
But all is in his hand whose praise I seek.
In vain the poet sings, and the world hears,
If he regard not, though divine the theme.
'Tis not in artful measures, in the chime,
And idle tinkling of a minstrel's lyre,
To charm his ear, whose eye is on the heart;
Whose frown can disappoint the proudest strain,
Whose approbation....PROSPER EVEN MINE.

Lightning Source UK Ltd.
Milton Keynes UK
UKHW020627120123
415223UK00007B/912